No Crisis f

Terence Sackett is a writer and
designer living in Somerset.
Look for his other books on Amazon

Terence Sackett

No Crisis for Hut Man

Bincombe Books

I live in a hut in the woods. Bernhard said it's a shed because boring men have sheds, and I'm not only a boring man, I'm a boring little man. I said I don't think so, Bernhard, sheds are at the bottom of gardens and I live in the woods. And, anyway, Sally doesn't think I'm boring.

My hut leaks so I banged nails in the roof to make it watertight. When I stretched the felt it broke into strips like the pasta Sally makes. I don't think they'd taste very nice like Sally's.

I use a pencil to write, not pens. What I write's there, and when I rub it with a bread crust it's not. If I feel peckish I pick up all the crumbs and eat my words. You don't waste food. The better I get at writing the better I think they'll taste.

I won't say where my hut is. It's down a combe, or up one, depending which way you're coming or going. Things can get complicated.

I think I think hard, but how can I know?

Whichever way, I'm along a track, through a gate that bangs you on the foot when it doesn't know you, past a holiday cottage with a trampoline and a funny looking tent where people do something called Glamping, and along a muddy path. Then into trees.

And that's where I am.

Sally's coming next week.

Sometimes I'd like to turn into a tree. Trees are good. I'd spread my arms and feel the sap rising, and fill my head with green. I'd be an apple tree and make fruit I could sell. But not an oak making acorns, I'm not a squirrel. Green's good.

I like mauve too.

We've got drips. I've moved my table with my boxes to the far end where there's more roof felt. I try hard to like drips, it's important, as they're being drips and just doing what they do. Sometimes when I get up I find shiny dents in the floor. They've gone off somewhere by lunchtime. I think rainwater turns into air, which is intriguing.

We're in a corner of a bumpy field that belongs to Sally's neighbours. They had it for a pony that died. They don't know I'm here but Sally does. I like Sally. Very much. Luckily they're old and walk with sticks so I think they've forgotten about it. And their dead pony. Old people don't remember much. Dad can't remember where he left his socks. Or who mum is sometimes. Poor dad.

I've friends here – Billy, Nils, and Nita – so I'm not alone. They don't say much. Billy's a bookcase, Nils a chair, and Nita a pair of curtains. After a difficult start we get on. I call them by their names. Why not? That's what

2

they call themselves on the cardboard packs. I say Time to shut up shop, Nita, and I pull her across the window. She's a bit long and picks up dust, but it's no crisis. I'm no good with a needle, and I've told Nita she'll have to stay too long. We all have to adapt, even curtains.

Sometimes I say Let's choose a book, Billy, I'll read that Penguin on your top shelf. Billy wobbles on the bumpy floor when I tug the Penguin out, but he doesn't mind. Nils doesn't mind being use as a table either. I don't talk to Nils as much as the other two.

I've brewed a cuppa.

My friends came in what they call Flat Packs. I carried them along the path to the wood from the lane. A man Sally knows called Bernhard left them in his room when he left her and she gave them to me.

Poor Sally.

Sally got me a job. She knew the girl who brought dead plants back to life at the garden centre who was sacked. A man in a green coat told me I didn't look old enough to take on the responsibility of watering important plants, but I told him Excuse me, I'm nineteen and a half.

Actually I was eighteen but I'm nineteen and a half now.

I've saved money I got working at the garden centre to buy things to live on extra to my benefit. People are funny. They asked what this bush was and if this plant liked sun or shade, and if it liked wet weather or dry. How should I know? I said a bit of both, it can't be far wrong. We all do. Plants can't be much different.

I got the hose twisted once and an old lady tripped and fell down. I think she was disabled before. I put her plant in the ambulance with her. I don't think she paid for it, but it's no loss. Patients like plants by their bed, even if it was one of the dead plants I brought back to life. I hope the doctors brought the old lady back to life too. I got sacked.

When I unpacked the Flat Packs Billy, Nils and Nita didn't look like themselves. I used a little key with a funny square top and now they look just like the drawings. Billy looks like Billy and settled in straight away. Like Nita he's a bit tall, so his top shelf's jammed under the roof and he slumps a bit. I use Nils the chair as a table sometimes. He's low like our family's coffee table, but I don't drink coffee. He's got a bump down the middle like chairs have for where the two sides of your bottom go, so he's better as the chair he is in the picture, but he'll have to adapt. We all do. I've used the cardboard packs as carpets.

So here we are. Our new life together.

We're hidden away in holly. Dogs bother me, they snuffle and sniff and get everywhere. I've got a catapult, and shoot pebbles when they get nosey. I pinged a spaniel this morning. It yelped and ran off and didn't come back.

Yesterday a woman came up the track. I was worried, it only takes one. She needed to wee. I wouldn't have picked holly to wee in so she must have really wanted one. I crept into the trees and made snake noises. S-s-s-s-s. She pulled her knickers up quick and I didn't see her again. She had white hair and was too old for me to want to peek at her parts.

I won't shoot humans with my catapult. Shooting's not polite or very Useful to Society, it makes nurses busy

4

in hospitals and they're busy enough already.

This is the only life I've got if the non-believers are right. It's my life and I want it to be exactly how it is. Christians who believe in another up in the sky I don't approve of. Some of them have big cars and houses like Mr Pearson who keeps a Bible poking out of his pocket that everyone can see. They cheat in their businesses, sell people things they don't want during the week, do things with people who aren't their wives or husbands, then make it better at church on Sundays.

I search for things that live on other things with dad's microscope. I prise off bits of oak bark and look at them under the glass. Then I turn up the magnification, and find another intriguing world.

I watch things move for hours, creatures with tiny waving legs and snouts and twisty feelers. Where are they going? Where do they think they're going? How should I know? But it's somewhere very small as they must breathe, otherwise they'd die. Their lungs must be small, too. Air must be even smaller to be small enough to get into their lungs. Lots of things are small when you stop looking at big things with the naked eye. All the big things you see are made of tiny bits you can't.

I've talked to Billy and he doesn't mind me using his top shelf for storing some of the interesting things I find living on other things. He's shiny and plastic and doesn't mind a bit of slime.

What now?

I don't sleep well because I watch for invaders.

Invaders come at any time, they don't work nine to five. Day and night don't mean much in the woods. Sometimes my day is night and sometimes the other way round, and I eat my dinner at three in the morning and my sugar snapcrackles at teatime. Who sets what a day is in stone? Not me.

I've been feeling sad, which I don't very often, because Ken the iguana died. He was green with black stripes and talked to me by bobbing his head. I've no idea what he was saying but he was probably telling me how happy he was living in the combe with me. He liked climbing trees and snapping at insects, even if he was a vegetarian.

A month ago when I was coming back from the shop on Lars with Ken on the handlebars I had to jam on the brakes going round a corner and bumped into some lady walkers. Ken fell off and got mangled in the spokes. He looked up at me and bobbed his head twice. I think he was telling me I couldn't be his friend any longer because he was dying.

And he did.

I fed Ken vegetables. I'd cycle down to the village shop on Lars with Ken on the handlebars. He'd sit on my shoulder while I bought food for him.

I asked the shopkeeper for lots of exotic things my iguana booklet told me Ken would like eating – mangos, papayas, snap peas, romaine lettuces. The shopkeeper said cabbage and carrots would have to do, as he wasn't bloody Tesco.

Sometimes the shop was busy and there were long queues, but everyone left when they saw Ken and I got to the front straightaway.

I'd say to Ken Do you fancy broccoli, Ken? He'd bob his head to say Yes or No.

One day I found two Kens in the hut and I thought he'd Propagated himself like the Virgin Mary did with Jesus. But he'd just shed his skin, and there was another Ken exactly the same underneath.

I went to see Sally to tell her how sad I was. She bought me a new plastic Ken, so it was no crisis. I think she said it came from the Amazon, which is where iguanas live. Which is very quick as it arrived the next day. I don't really believe it did come all that way, but Sally isn't a liar so I'm not sure. I'm great friends with the new Ken, and it's good as I don't need to feed him or worry about him not getting enough sun. I still talk to him like I did to the old Ken, but he can't bob his head and answer because he's plastic.

We all have to adapt.

Sometimes when it's sunny I wear dark glasses during the day. I found a pair on the path. I think a lady hiker dropped them because they're purple with gold sparkles. Things look like night through them even in the day, but that's because they're dark themselves. It's no crisis because I'm sensible and I just use them for looking when it's sunny.

I wouldn't sell dark glasses in Greenland. Half the year you wouldn't sell any because Nature makes it dark. Maybe shops there sell twice as many pairs in summer to make up. I've thought hard about this but I doubt it, because people can only wear one pair at a time. Maybe shops in Greenland sell fish instead in summer, you eat fish whether it's light or dark. I do.

I like fish fingers.

It's holiday time. Not mine, my life's a holiday. I like being alone but I'm very interested in walkers, you can't miss them in their bright anoraks. I ignored them first. Now I like catching their attention, but I do it away from my hut. Why? To intrigue them. I like that word Intrigue. It makes things interesting, which they are. And not just for me – I want to make their lives as intriguing and interesting as mine.

What do these people do when they ask themselves What to do now? Watch a video, eat a doughnut, do some shopping, clean the car? Or cry. I bet a lot have a good cry when they think how sad their lives are. It's a shame they don't have friends they can rely on like Billy, Nils and Nita.

More drips, lots of them. The Flat Pack carpets are soft like mouldy biscuits so water's coming up through the mud floor.

Poor Nils caught foot rot like sheep. I got dad's saw out I took from his shed, turned him over, and said This is going to hurt you more than it hurts me, Nils. I hacked an inch off his bad foot. It wasn't a proper cut and a bit crooked, so I went round each leg three times, cutting them more level each time till he stopped wobbling. I have to bend down to Nils now when I want to write or eat, and sometimes my plate slides off and I have to scoop up my fish fingers from the floor. But it's no crisis, what's dust when it's at home? Everything's made of dust, including me. I'm made of Electrons and Particles and other tiny things the Creator of the Universe has stuck together. He's clever.

I walked to the stream this morning and the sun came out and I wrote a poem about it. I wrote how it dusted the pebbles in the shallows. Can the sun dust? It's liquid in one way and air in another. But I don't think it's proper dust. And I wrote that water in the stream splashes light. Can light splash? Or is it the water? Writers write about things by saying they look like other things. Lambs look like feather dusters, and birds and skies like fishes and water. But they aren't, are they? Things are better staying themselves, that's how we know what they are. What's the point in writing about a bee and saying it's not a bee but a striped humbug?

Breakfast time. I'm sitting on Nils crunching a Ryvita. In my head it sounds like explosions like in dad's film about the War.

Another dog snuffled this way this afternoon, maybe he heard me crunching my Twix. I fired my catapult at him and he yelped and ran off.

Sally came. She didn't stay long.

I like watching the stream. It's on its way somewhere. Somewhere that's elsewhere and not here.

Water's intriguing. It's always the same but different. When I toss a stick into the steam it catches on a rock, as if it likes being just where it is and doesn't want to move anywhere else. Water never catches or snags, which is intriguing. When I think hard about it I see it pouring into the pond down by the hotel, then flowing out into the sea where it becomes something else, but still water but filled with salt. Salt's a bit like dust. You can't see it when it's in the sea, only in the packets you buy at the shop.

Sticks look bent in water but straight when you take them out. I don't think water really bends things. I've thought about it a lot because a stick can't be in and out of the water at the same time, so how can you tell? Sticks may be cleverer than we think.

We've stopped talking. But I think they're still talking to each other, Billy, Nils and Nita. I hear them when I listen at the door, but they stop when I come into the hut.

I've got a limp. I don't want to prop myself straight like Billy the bookcase – I can't walk with Penguins strapped to my foot like him. And I don't want to chop my leg shorter like I did to Nils to make me level. You have to be sensible about these things.

Walking down hills I'd need more Penguins, and my rucksack's full already with Twix bars, cheese triangles, Ken the plastic iguana, a compass, my fossil kipper, and pyjamas in case I get lost. Where would the surgeon cut? Lop off my foot, take a bit out of the ankle, sew the foot back on? Or cut off the other foot and add a new ankle? And where would they get a new ankle? I don't think there's a donor list.

Would I want a shorter leg or a longer one? To be taller or shorter? Neither. I like myself exactly the height I am, I know where the world is at five foot two. I'd ask Billy what he thinks. But they only talk to each other,

Billy, Nils and Nita. Probably in Swedish, because that's where they come from.

This morning I saw some walkers in the combe. They were standing where the path forks and goes off in two different directions. One of them was going on and on in a sing song voice about taking the path not taken, and wondering where the other one went and how Not Taking it Might Have Affected His Life. It's important to help people so I went over and told him that actually both paths went round in a circle and met up at the same place so it wouldn't have made any difference. He looked cross and said he was actually reciting a famous poem. I told him I wanted to be a poet but hadn't written a whole one yet as I was still rubbing my words out with a bread crust. Then they all looked cross and walked off along the Road More Taken. You can't please everyone.

Yesterday on the hill I wanted to be a cloud. Not because they're damp and fluffy, but because they don't have to think which way they're going. The wind tells them. I'd like that, unless it blew me somewhere I didn't want to go and I'd have to wait for a change in the weather to get back. I'd have to take my pyjamas. And I'd probably run out of cheese triangles.

When I think hard I want to be exactly where I am, and not be a cloud. They're going one way quite happily then suddenly it's Whoaaaa, wind's turned, hang on, we're off somewhere else. Like a mystery tour that goes on and on and on.

Clouds don't really have much choice, and choice is everything in my life. If I want to stay in bed I stay in bed. But being a cloud is a good way to make friends. They join together in the sky and sail off arm in arm. Clouds like the wind, but I don't, I plug holes in the hut to keep it out. It makes the pasta strips on the roof slap and sound like we're being attacked by birds like the film I watched at Aunt Megs when she looked shocked and put the cover over her budgie cage just in case.

Today I'm measuring things. I like to understand everything exactly, and I'm starting in the hut because this is where I live.

First I measure Nils, then Billy, then Nita. I'm using a stick, as I haven't got a ruler. I've marked the stick in small measuring bits with a pen. Everything I measure is a stick and a bit or a stick and two bits or three. Not many things are exactly one stick long or two sticks long. Which is intriguing. Most things must be odd.

Maybe my stick's a funny length. How can I find this out? I'll measure some other places. You can't know too much about what things measure. Dad said it's important to get the measure of things in life and that's what I always do.

If I worry about anything it's that I've missed people who've come to visit. I've no door knocker. Sally banged on the window when she came, but she knows me and I was waiting for her anyway. The other people who called wouldn't bang hard even if there was a knocker as they don't know me and it would be rude. So who called? The prime minister, Cliff Richard? Who knows? It's rude not to be in.

Do door knockers hear themselves knocking? If they do it won't worry them much because it's what they do.

Today I disguised myself as a pile of leaves and lay by the path in the wood. I don't think anyone spotted me as no one said There's a pile of leaves with a small man in. Once when I was a pile of leaves two lots of people passed.

One said, well, that's our exercise done for the day, now for the cream tea.

And another said That'll undo all the good work, and they both laughed.

Sally says it's called Repartee.

I don't really understand Repartee. I'd like to learn exactly what to say back to people when they say things to me. I'm thinking of writing things down they might say in my notebook and thinking up things to reply. It won't be a long list. No one's going to talk about football or how to get to the Co-op here in the woods.

Maybe if I say something first I can leave it to them to think of something to reply. That would be easier.

Today I cycled to the butcher in the village to buy some corned beef. I like corned beef. I eat it on Ryvita biscuits. They explode when I bite them so I put a piece of toilet paper on my knees to scoop up the crumbs. Then I feed the birds with them. I pick out the bits of corned beef in case the birds are vegetarians.

There was another man with a limp like mine at the counter. His was on the right foot, mine's on the left. We'd look very odd if we walked along together, so I wouldn't want him as a friend. He kept waving his arms and talking very loud and pointing at the meat in the window like that actor in Shakespeare I saw with Sally. I'm trying hard to remember what he said because it was intriguing. I think he said the meat cuts rippled in waves across the trays. And the chops flickered like frames in a Polish film. I haven't seen a Polish film so how should I know. Then he said the topside with string tied round it was like spirals round the Trajan column. I thought a Trajan was an old motorbike. But maybe that's a Trojan.

I think the Trojans were Greeks. A lot of things are more than one thing, which can be confusing.

When he got his purse out to pay, the man with the limp said The inclined legs of mutton look like the Acropolis, which I think is in Greece and a very old building whose walls have fallen down. The butcher didn't say a word, so maybe he doesn't understand Repartee either. Or he'd never been to Greece. Maybe the man with the limp said lots of things like that in the shop before and the butcher got fed up and gave him his limp with his meat cleaver. I would, he held us up.

My bike's called Lars.

I do everything fast.
But
sometimes
I
do
every
thing
very
slow
ly

It's my choice, after all, and choice is everything in a perfect life like mine.

Sometimes when I walk up the combe I say to myself, You're a mouse. When I'm a mouse I walk slowly, thinking Mouse. But mice move very fast indeed but don't travel very far at all. Walking like a mouse is what's called an Exercise in Imagination. It's never a long walk for me, but it would be for a mouse. If I really walked like a mouse I'd get back very early and have lots of time to do something else. Which is good as I am very busy.

When I'm walking like a mouse I think hard and try to see the world like a mouse. I sniff the grass and peer up through the trees looking for buzzards and anything else big that will try to kill me. Being a mouse makes everything intriguing, and mice must lead quite interesting lives. But a bit short, as I'd be born one year and probably die the next.

Once I thought I'd walk as slow as a snail, but didn't, as it would have been a very short walk and I'd hardly have got to the path in the combe before it was dark and time to head home. You have to be sensible about these things.

Whenever I'm a mouse and I hear a bike or a rambler I hide in the holly and keep sniffing. Mice never stop sniffing the world. They don't mind sniffing things I don't think are very nice, like rubbish heaps and scraps of old potato and meat with fungus on.

I think what smells nice is different depending on who you are. I don't like the smell of dog poo, but Sally's spaniel Kevin does. Why? Because we are all different, which is the Wonder of God's Universe. And it means there's nothing in the world that's really horrible if someone you like likes it. I like Kevin, Sally's dog, even if I don't like the things he does or sniffs. I let Kevin sniff and lick my face even if he has just been licking dog poo. It's a bit disgusting, but I don't want to upset Sally by saying her dog is.

I wonder how my face smells to Kevin. Who knows? I think Sally's face would smell nice, and Kevin must think it does because he's always sniffing and licking it when I'm there. I don't know how I could find out. I'm not a dog so I can't jump on Sally's lap and sniff and lick her. I wish I could.

Today I'm using Nils as a table not a chair. I'm writing poetry, and a table like Nils, though he's really a chair, is just the right size for a small poem.

Wordworth's a poet. He probably wrote his poem about daffodils on a table when he got back home after Wandering Lonely as a Cloud. But not a Flat Pack table like Nils because in Wordworth's time the Swedes were probably still Vikings, raping and pillaging and not making furniture.

If I was writing a big, sad Russian book like Mr Tolstoy I'd choose a dining table like mum and dad's, because Russian books are very heavy. Mr Tolstoy's are. Two of three would probably break Billy's shelves. But I'm not, and if I was I'd have to wait till I was really in the glooms. My life's too perfect to write a Russian book.

Writers say everything must be exactly right when they start writing. Otherwise they listen to Woman's Hour or tidy the under stairs cupboard. I'm keeping an old toilet roll I found in mum and dad's under stairs cupboard just in case I do get the glooms and want to go on and on and on for hundreds and hundreds of pages about how awful everything is. It's too shiny to wipe my bottom with.

I'm using my pencil and a bread crust rubber for my poem, because poets don't write pages full of sentences, they pick away at their poem because it's already there on the paper. They just rub away to get to it. Which is reassuring. But already I've had to buy another loaf to rub away with and still haven't got far with my poem.

Maybe I've got writer's block. Can you get writer's block when you haven't even started? I hope so.

I like pound shops. With ten pounds you buy ten things. What's easier? Ten things are better than five or six. I wish the village shop was a pound shop. Buying one thing there always costs more than a pound, especially my sugar snapcrackles, corned beef or cheese triangles.

A lady passed me today in the combe. She said Good Morning! And I said Good morning! but just after in case I interrupted her. I nodded, which is polite. I like looking at ladies. Not out of the corner of my eye like some men do, which is rude. I look straight at them, which is the best thing to do with most things, including ladies.

When I looked at her she looked at me and We Caught Each Other's Eye, then I looked away. Otherwise that's rude too. You mustn't stare, especially at ladies you don't know, they might think you're undressing them, which is what Bernhard did with ladies, even ones old enough to be his mother. Sally always got cross with him. Lots of things are rude that people don't recognize. It's why the world is such an unhappy place for so many people.

Catch her eye. An intriguing phrase. I looked at a lady once at the garden centre. She was pushing her trolley round the hardy perennials. When she saw I'd caught her eye I held out my hand and gave it back and she looked startled. But I had got one of her eyes, so it probably wasn't surprising. Not at all, I said, though she hadn't thanked me for giving it back. She didn't hand mine back, so maybe only one eye gets caught at a time, even though we had four between us. Who chooses which eye gets caught? It's intriguing. After I'd handed her eye back we didn't say anything else. She pushed her trolley on to the hydrangeas and I filled my watering can to bring some more dead plants back to life.

I like dreamy days.

What's a dreamy day? Lying on Sally's sofa sinking into her spotted cushions listening to her Japanese music. And eating the biscuits she buys for me. Sometimes they're bourbons and sometimes those with jam in the middle that look like the Bishop of Somewhere's dahlias at the garden centre. I say I'll think I'll have a dahlia today, please Sally.

And we both laugh.

I think Sally must have bought the biscuits specially for me, but as I'm not at Sally's when I'm not there I can't really say. I hope she did.

Once quite a long time ago when I went round there was another man lying on Sally's sofa. I couldn't see any biscuits and she didn't offer me any. Nor a cup of tea. Which is unlike Sally. She had her dressing gown on and told me to come back next Thursday. The man didn't have his trousers or shirt on, just his underpants. Maybe she was doing his washing and ironing, Sally's kind like that. That man was Bernhard.

Sally's Japanese music isn't really music, just screams and screeches. She says it's played on violins. Why use a violin when it doesn't sound like one? It's like using a fork as a spoon. The screams and screeches sound more like drills at the dentist than music.

Once when I was dreamily listening Sally told me to close my mouth or I'd catch a fly. No flies on me, Sally, I said, and we laughed.

We laugh a lot, Sally and me.

I want to be an entertainer, but you need to learn jokes just like I'm learning Repartee. I've written out some jokes from crackers and I practice on Billy, Nils and Nita. They don't laugh, but they are Swedish.

Sally's Japanese music is a bit like being at the dentist. But I think the Japanese have good teeth so it probably wouldn't remind them of the dentist. It's called Cultural Diversity.

I prefer drum music and military bands. But I don't tell Sally, I like her sofa and biscuits too much. And I like Sally, but I don't tell her that either.

I've just bought some wipes. You tug each one out of a little flap then press it flat again. They're slimy and wet, but not with water. I've been worried about my relationship with Billy and Nils. Maybe they think I'm not looking after them properly, so I thought I'd do what the packet says: For a beautiful shine give them a Wipe and Go.

Which is curious. Why go anywhere after you've

wiped? And go where? Once you've wiped, everything's clean and comfortable, and you'd want to stay not go. Otherwise, what's the point?

I've been thinking hard. Why go anywhere at all? Zen monks don't. They never leave their room. Nothing wrong with being here, they tell themselves, might as well sit tight. They cross their legs, close their eyes, but still travel all the way to the Source of the Universe without moving a muscle.

Travelling in your head's cheap. And you don't have to take your pyjamas. All it costs is time, and not much of that because Zen monks travel in what's called the Eternal Present. I'm not sure where this is so I need to go to the library.

You can travel faster in your head than in the fastest plane. I can be here one moment and in Chile or China the next. You're somewhere else before you know it, with no risk of crashing or injuries or dying. You don't have to wait in queues, or wait for your luggage to come round, or book hotels, or have malaria jabs. You're just there, which is like being at home but not.

I put my bathing trunks on once and travelled in my head to somewhere called Ibiza that Sally told me she went with Bernhard. They took all their clothes off to sunbathe on the beach, which was quite rude. I felt embarrassed when I did it in the hut, even though I was on my own. I got sunburn, which was curious, because it was winter and very cold. So I had some mango squash and went to Bridlington instead.

And if you don't like where you are you aren't stuck there for a fortnight. You just choose somewhere else.

It's when your body does the travelling that problems start. Maybe Zen monks are wiser than we thought. They travel Zen not Easyjet.

Today Lars and I came back from the village on a lane I'd never used before. His spokes pinged because my coat kept getting caught in the wheel. It was like Sally's Japanese music but more musical.

Ping, ping, ping, ping.

I'd like to play my Lars music to Sally, but we'd have to be on a tandem together and Lars has only got one very small saddle. On the way back to the hut I puffed a lot and had to stop when Lars's chain came off from all the pinging.

I saw a little wooden house on stilts in the trees. A green flag was flying. It could mean Come in for tea and cake, or Beware mad dog. How could I know?

A sign on the door said Knock here. So I did.

Who's that knocking? someone called. Come in if you must, I can't get to the door.

The man from the butchers with a limp on the other leg from mine who called the meat display a Polish film was sitting on the floor. He was throwing dice.

You saw the flag?

Yes.

The red one?

The green one.

My red flag's green?

Yes.

Hells bells, it's meant to be red, he said. Green means I'm in and red I'm out, even when I'm in. Look, I've got a lot on. I've just thrown thirty six double sixes in a row.

My record's forty-two. If I'd heard a car I'd have nipped out and changed the flags over.

I told him I came by bike.

Bike! Good Lord, I'll need to work on that, it could ruin my work cycle – pun intended. I'll scatter tacks on the drive. Go on, shoo.

And I did.

Sally's dog would have had its tail between its legs but luckily I don't have one. Nor does Sally's dog.

Not a nice person. I won't cycle his way again.

Where do we all come from? And when did we get here?

I think a lot about it, it's intriguing. But I don't let it bother me. Because wherever it was it happened a long time ago, as the Universe is ancient. Even the oldest people with the longest memories can't tell us. Even mum and dad's friend Aunt Megs didn't know, and she was very old. Maybe she'd forgotten. Last time I was there just before she died she called me Heather.

None of my Penguins tell me where we come from. Nor the books at the library. I asked the librarian, but when we looked there was only a children's book and it said we were flown here by storks. I don't think so, you have to be sensible. Children probably know better than us, because they've only just come from wherever it is.

Some people think the drawings of mummies on stones will tell us. Professors say they've broken the code, but how do we know they know? How do they know they know? The pictures might just be telling us how Egyptians cut their toenails or what they fed their camels.

Wherever we came from is probably a very long way

away. But when I think hard it could be somewhere quite close. Time doesn't have much to do with distance.

Have I been here before? To this hut? How should I know? But I do know why I'm here. I'm here because Trevor and Eileen propagated me. I used that word a lot working at the garden centre. It's not rude. Trevor and Eileen are mum and dad. I call them Trevor and Eileen now I've left home, but actually they're not at home any longer, they're in a Home.

A curious word Home for a place where people live who aren't living at home any longer.

I call mum and dad mum and dad but they aren't my real parents and didn't propagate me. But they have been for as long as I can remember. They look more like a nan and granddad, but it's no crisis. They're kind! And always have been.

Sometimes when I phone the Home I forget to ask for Trevor and Eileen and ask the nurse for mum and dad. She probably doesn't know which ones I want to speak to. She asks which ones because there are fifty mums and dads to choose from. Sometimes I think she takes the phone to the wrong mum and dad. But how I can I tell, I'm not there to see. It's no crisis, because at least someone's mum and dad are being talked to. Maybe someone else's son talks to Trevor and Eileen when they call, so it balances out. In a way I don't mind, because they're both deaf, especially Trevor, and it takes almost all of the phone call just to say Hello and to tell them it's me their son calling. Usually the nurse does most of the talking, but it's difficult to talk to her because she's very nice but foreign. Not only are all these mums and dads not living at home but it must feel like living in a

23

foreign country with foreign voices telling them it's their son phoning.

I think Trevor and Eileen are usually asleep when I call and don't hear very much. They don't seem to mind. How could they if they're asleep?

All these mums and dads and nans and granddads look exactly the same because they're old and asleep most of the time. The nurse must have name tags to tell the difference.

Sometimes I like to do something very difficult. I'm trying to stop my fingernails growing. Why do nails grow? They don't need to. I don't have to catch mice with them like buzzards, and I use a knife to cut up my fish fingers. Why does God waste His time making nails grow? There are much more important things for him to do in this world, especially as He has to be everywhere doing everything all the time.

I've been concentrating, saying Stop growing nails, stay exactly how long you are. But God's more powerful than me, He made the Universe. Maybe I need to concentrate harder. But not too hard as they may stop growing completely and I'd have ugly stumps instead.

I noticed something strange about my nails yesterday. What's called the moon poking through at the bottom of my little finger is tiny. But the moons on my thumbs get bigger and bigger till they're almost as big as half moons. Do nails grow and shrink like the moon with the tides? Why not? We don't know why God does all the things He does.

I don't think I've stopped them growing yet, but I cut them last week so it's hard to tell.

I'd like to stop my toenails growing, too, but I've got socks on so they can't see me telling them not to grow.

I'll stick to my fingernails, ten's quite enough to think about.

Something intriguing and worrying happened today. When I got back from my walk there were two men with cameras in the hut.

They wore narrow trousers like dad's old drainpipes, and pointed shoes with chunks of mud on. It serves them right for not wearing hiking boots. They said I was an Opportunity not to be Missed.

The man called Eddie, who talked like Sally's friend Cosmo, moved Penguins from Billy's shelves on to Nils, making tidy piles. He said he was the stylist. I thought he said Cyclist and asked where his bike was and they laughed. They liked my joke, so I think I'm getting better as an entertainer.

They want to feature my hut in their Interior Design Magazine. I asked why, and the man called Jeremy said Your hut's an outstanding example of an Open Plan Dynamic Interior. Eddie laughed and said it's Open Plan on Steroids.

Then they both laughed and I joined in because it's polite to laugh at other people's jokes, especially when they laugh at mine.

When I'm in their magazine I'd be Trending, they said, whatever that is. People will be coming miles to see my hut.

I can't have that.

Then they took more photos.

When they left I piled branches round the hut then

went out for a walk and couldn't find it when I got back.

No one's visited so I don't think I'm Trending yet. I've been watching the path.

They're not talking to me, Billy, Nils and Nita.

Nita's fallen off the wall. Now anyone coming to see me Trending can look through the window.

I didn't sleep well last night worrying about Trending. I looked it up in my dictionary. It means Currently Popular. I don't know how long Currently is but I've had enough of Trending and being Currently Popular already. I'm going camping before everyone starts arriving.

I'll visit my aunt in Cornwall. I've never been there and I hope she's still alive. She was when I visited mum and dad at the Home because there was a card from her with a Christmas robin on. But I hadn't been to see mum and dad for a while so it could have been a card from the Christmas before.

She's very old, my aunt. Or was. The writing on her card looks scrawly because old people's hands shake. She wrote Happy Christmas Trevor and Eileen. I hope mum and dad are still alive. I never know when I ring up the home because as I've already said I don't think the staff know which mum and dad I want to talk to. Poor mum and dad.

I'm getting the bus into town and I'm on my own at the stop.

I don't travel on buses in the country. Which is not surprising as they only come twice a day when I'm not

26

there and don't need them.

I hope no one brings a pig on the bus. It's what farmers do in the country, Bernhard told me. I've got a picture of one in an old Ladybird book. The timetable says the bus comes at 10.09.

It's not here yet because nothing happens when it says it does in the country. Cows and sheep aren't born at exactly 10.09 and sometimes not till a week later, so I hope farmers don't waste time waiting. Farmers are very busy like me. They do things I wouldn't like to do like poking their hands up cows' bottoms.

I'm thinking about how to catch the bus. Will it stop when it comes? It didn't the last time I tried and went straight past.

You Hail a bus. Otherwise you miss it and have to wait till tomorrow if it's the afternoon one.

Hail. An intriguing word. I'm practising Hailing while I wait. I wave my arm, which I think is what you do for Hailing, because country bus stops are not what are called Compulsory Stops.

Just now as I was practising Hailing a car came past and boys stuck their heads out of the window and laughed and threw an orange that hit my face.

Not very nice.

It's coming. It's green and racing towards me. I Hail it and it jerks to a halt like I've given it a surprise. I ask for the camping shop in Minehead and the driver says he'll let me out in the High Street. I sit on an outside seat in case a farmer tries to put a pig next to me.

So far so good. No pigs, not even a chicken.

We keep turning left then right as if it's the way to Minehead. Which it isn't, straight along the main road is much quicker. Maybe it's a new driver. It's like a fly buzzing along, this bus. It goes everywhere first before it gets to where it's supposed to be going. No wonder it's empty.

I wouldn't want to be a fly. They eat poo.

I'm changing my mind about going to Minehead as I didn't realize we'd have to go everywhere else first. I like staying still where I am, because Zen monks say Stillness is the Path to Wisdom.

Or I did before Jeremy and Eddie came with their cameras.

The camping store wasn't in the High Street at all. It took me an hour to find. It was miles out of town near a garden centre and a scrap yard. It was like a metal hut, but much bigger than mine.

Inside there were tents all over the floor, like a camp site without grass and trees and campers.

Where to start? How should I know?

A man came over and said How can I help you, sir? I told him I was going camping to visit my aunt in Cornwall.

We've a range of tents second to none, sir, he said. You're camping alone?

I think so, I said.

What else? But I made out I was thinking about it, otherwise it's rude.

Well, sir, he said, you never know when you're going to get lucky, do you, and winked.

I don't really know what winking means. I think it means You know what I mean.

I didn't, but I winked back to be polite.

He said Then you may not be ▮▮▮▮▮▮▮ e-man tent, sir, and winked again. It was too ▮▮▮▮▮top him because he was already showing me some bigger tents.

This one's just the job, he said. Easy pitch, cross pole for extra strength, with no way in for unwanted draughts, moisture or bugs. Room for a very cosy two, I'd say. And he winked again.

I looked inside and winked back and said it was very roomy – Open Plan on Steroids, in fact, and he laughed. I like sharing jokes, you don't need to keep thinking up new ones. I don't think Jeremy the stylist would mind.

Right, sleeping bags, he said. They come in mummy shape, square, pod, down, or synthetic. This Eventer 450's ideal. Durable fabric, multi-fibre insulation, drawcord, internal zip baffle, deep pocket for those essentials. We'll look at doubles, shall we, he said, and winked again. Before I could wink back he'd walked off saying, Wait here, sir.

I sat in the tent planning how I'd fit Billy, Nils and Nita in it even though they're not coming with me, while he went round and round the store three times. He came back with a trolley full of camping stuff.

Right, sir. Two-man tent, pod sleeping bag, mallet, gas stove, cool box, water container, plates, cutlery, lantern, everything you need. And to you, sir, an exclusive one-day only price for the package. A very special £225 with your one-off unique discount and prestige club membership. Cash or card, sir?

I told him all I wanted to buy were some tent pegs and a plastic knife and fork. He looked cross.

Well, we won't be going far on that, will we, chummy? Anyway, we're closing, vacate the premises NOW.

And he █████████ his drainpipes. Not a nice man, especially after █████████ red winks and jokes. You can never tell, can you?

It's late and I've missed the bus back to the hut so I'll have to stay somewhere. I haven't brought my pyjamas.

Choosing a B&B is difficult. There are lots down by the harbour but how can I tell which one? They all say the same on their signs – Bed and Breakfast, En-suite, which I think is French, and TV in all rooms. Except one near the end that says Boutique B&B. It must be a ladies' shop where you can stay the night. But I don't want to buy a dress or brassiere, just a bed and breakfast.

I'd prefer to buy a dress for Sally than a brassiere. I haven't measured Sally, because it would be impolite. I think brassiere measuring's done with cups, but for women like mum mugs would be better. Is it a ladies only B&B? It must be, as men don't shop in boutiques. Dad didn't. Men buy clothes in shops called Outfitters with blazers, striped ties and jumpers with coloured diamonds in the window.

Another B&B said it was a Restaurant with Rooms. I should think so, that's what's called Stating the Obvious.

I chose this B&B because it's got a happy face. Why stay in a house that looks grumpy? I don't take chances with my night's sleep.

I'm in a room at the top of the house. The plumbing gurgles. A lady in a frilly housecoat with a spot on her chin I tried hard not to stare at showed me up.

She said Follow me, Young Man.

I said Thank you, Old Lady, and she got cross and said

Don't be rude.

We turned right up the stairs, pushed through a fire door, up more stairs, turned left, up more stairs, pushed through another fire door, and it was the last room on the left but one. We must have walked nearly all the way back to the hut.

Seven o'clock. I'm tired. Early to bed. The bed's got slithery sheets that crackle like firework sparklers. I hitch the blanket up over my nose because it makes the air you breathe warm and cosy. I'm reading my book about rabbits. Rabbits are intriguing. It's a short book, and in the first picture there are only two rabbits and on the last page hundreds.

Sometimes I wish Sally was a rabbit, but if she was she'd be breeding all the time and her flat would be full of rabbits and she'd get evicted.

I've got a photo of Sally. I keep it in my book on rabbits and look at her when I read it. Sally's cuddly, but not furry. Not the bits of her I've seen.

I hope I'll wake up in time for breakfast. 8.30 the old lady said, nine o'clock, latest. There's no clock, but dad said if you tap your head eight times, son, you wake up on the dot. What about 8.30? How do I do half a tap? A tap's a tap, you have to be sensible about these things. I don't want to miss breakfast, as Mum says it's the most important meal of the day and sets you up so you can do more things. Unless you're old. Mum and dad always eat breakfast in their Home and all they do is sleep and watch telly.

The walls here make noises. There's water flowing through pipes inside them and electricity running through wires.

Electricity's there but it's not, which is intriguing. I tried looking for it once and smelt the plug, but you only know it's there when it gives you a shock. Luckily electricity can't get out of its wires like water. Water gets out of pipes and goes everywhere. I read that snakes can live in pipes, but they'd have to be thin like worms.

When I'm in bed at night in the hut owls tap at the window. They hoot and poke the glass with their beaks so I pull Nita tight across the window. I think they're friendly, but I'm not sure. Lots of things that are friendly during the day don't seem friendly at night, including trees that suddenly look like monsters.

They've got what they call Fire Doors here but they won't keep snakes out if they're in the pipes. They say Keep Shut in big red letters and close without you telling them to, so I'm safe from fires but not snakes.

I've woken up. What's the time? Time for breakfast?

I haven't slept much. I don't think I got enough ozone. Ozone's the special air at the seaside that makes you healthy. It must have salt in it like the sea, otherwise you'd get it everywhere else too. My window wouldn't open properly so I only got two inches of ozone. I think a foot of it would have given me more sleep.

I don't wash my down below parts, just my face in case I'm late. Then I go downstairs through a fire door, through the corridor, down some stairs, turn right, down more stairs, through a fire door, round a corner, and down stairs to eat my breakfast.

The dining room's busy. Am I late? The clock on the wall says 9.15. The Old Lady's cross and tells me I'll have to be quick as chef is going home. I sit by the window and look at the menu. I choose lamb cutlets and roast potatoes then spotted dick. I usually have sugar snapcrackles.

Time to leave and go home. I wave goodbye to the Old Lady. She says You're not staying then, young man? I'm not reducing the tariff.

Tariff. An intriguing word. I'll look it up in my dictionary.

I practice my Repartee on a man and a woman looking at tourist leaflets in the hall.

Where are you off to? I ask. Sunbathing?

Telly and bed, they say.

Which is curious. Why waste a day at the seaside watching telly and sleeping?

I walk down to the harbour. People at the pub are sitting outside eating their breakfasts. Pubs open very early at the seaside, it must be the ozone.

At the bus stop I wait but the bus doesn't come. It's getting dark. I think the sun's going in, not coming out. Which is intriguing. A man tells me there's no point in waiting, chum, the bus went hours ago.

We must be witnessing an eclipse, I tell him. When's the next bus?

Tomorrow, he says.

This service is even worse than I thought. I'll have to hitch home. Which means more Hailing, which I think I'm getting very good at.

It's dark when I get out of town. I stand by the roundabout but only two cars pass and a lorry in twenty minutes. They all drive by. It's dark, darker than the combe.

At last a car stops. It's a police car.

Where are you off to, young man?

Home to my hut.

Where's that, then?

The combe.

A long way to walk on a dark night, sir.

I think you'll find it's morning, officer, I tell him.

Been drinking, sir?

Mango squash.

They look at each other.

Get in, they say, we'll drive you home.

They tell me it's still Today, not Tomorrow. I'm confused. It's Today to me, but my Today is their Yesterday. And their Tomorrow will be my Today. I explain this carefully to the policemen, who seem what's called a Little Slow on the Uptake. They lock the doors and drive faster. I'm getting home quick and it's still Yesterday. I've saved a day, which is useful as I'm very busy. I've got all Tomorrow now and not just what's left of it from Today.

I spent all night in Accident and Emergency in Taunton. The nurse made me wear a back to front dress that showed my bottom. A man in a white coat and a tie with zebras on asked if I had a History of Mental Illness? Do I look like a library? I asked him. Not on Billy's shelves, I said. He gave me an injection and that's all I can remember.

I didn't have breakfast. An ambulance took me home.

I'll cycle to my aunt's. It's summer, so I'm packing dad's old tent, a sleeping bag and pyjamas, a jumper and a flannel. I'll tie them to the carrier on the back with my special stuff and dictionary.

I say goodbye to Billy, Nils and Nita.

I put my plastic money card in my pocket. It's got what's called a Pin. A Pin's a number that's special to me. I've remembered the number because it's dad's birthday back to front and a month behind. It gives me money through a slot called a Hole in the Wall. Dad gave it to me when he went into the home with mum. He said Here's some money, son, keep it for a rainy day.

Which is odd. Why keep money for when it's raining? You can't go out and you can't spend money at home. When I did want money once in Minehead it wasn't raining, which wasn't very helpful. And once when it was raining I'd forgotten to take my money card.

I think dad was already confused when he gave me the card. He was wearing odd socks and mum's pink cardigan. He spilt tea over his foot and stuffed most of his jam doughnut into mum's ear. I don't think they get on any more. Poor mum and dad.

Saturday afternoon. I'll leave tomorrow.

Lars and I cycled down to the village. I padlocked him to a lamp post and joined a queue outside the village hall.

I like queues, I practice my Repartee. Everyone was looking at their watches and getting cross about whatever was happening not happening on time. I sang Why Are We Waiting but no one joined in.

When the door opened we charged in like buffaloes in John Wayne films. I made horns with my fingers and mooed and butted the lady in front, but no one laughed except an old lady with a tea cosy on her head.

It was a jumble sale and a lady caught her skirt in the door rushing in and I saw her knickers. Another got trampled and needed first aid.

I like jumble sales. There's lots of stuff people don't want that other people do want before they get rid of it because they don't want it either. Like old jumpers and toys and toasters with bits of old crust in and grey underpants. I bought a mug with a picture of a monkey on, a Matchbox fire engine, and a bracelet for Sally. It's pink. I don't think the diamonds are real, but I can't be sure. You get bargains everywhere if you've got an eye like me.

A lady said You like books?

Is the Pope a catholic, I said.

I bought a book about hamsters for 5p. Hamsters are like mice but don't have tails. I bought a tin saucepan to cook in and wore it on my head like a helmet and marched out of the hall like a soldier. Eyes right! I shouted. At ease! Attention! Everyone laughed except for the old lady wearing a tea cosy who screamed Nazis! and hid under a table.

When I got outside something intriguing happened. In the front of the book about hamsters it said This book belongs to Helen. If you find it return it to Helen Jacobs, 33 Riverside Close, Budleigh Salterton.

Which was worrying, because it belonged to me now. But I know that ink writing means Things are for Ever, unless it's in pencil and you can rub it out. This was in red ink so whoever wrote it was saying I definitely want this book to belong to me Forever. You don't argue with red, especially at traffic lights. I don't.

So I'm not going to my aunt's in Cornwall, I'm off to Helen's in Budleigh Salterton to give her her book back. It's more important than visiting an aunt in Cornwall who may be dead anyway.

Where is Budleigh Salterton? I went back to the jumble sale and bought a road map book. It's old and doesn't have motorways, but I don't cycle up motorways or down them, so it's no crisis.

I looked at the road map book to see where Budleigh Salterton is and couldn't find it. I turned the pages and got all the way to Scotland and still didn't find it. I'd travelled 450 miles, much too far to pedal. Then I looked for my hut and found it on page 6. Then I found Budleigh Salterton at the bottom of page 5. Not far at all, just one page. It's by the sea in Devon which is quite next door to where I live compared to Scotland

When I say next door I don't mean Literally, it's what's called a Turn of Phrase. Which itself is an intriguing phrase.

I'm thinking of becoming a Student of the English language.

I probably won't cycle along the main road to Helen's, as lorries knock you off. I'll go everywhere first like the bus to Minehead because Lars and I are in no hurry and we don't have to be anywhere by 10.09.

I like lanes. They go like clouds go, just where they want to. They whizz along then suddenly say Ah, here's a field coming up, quick, turn left NOW. And they do, because they've no choice. Otherwise they go into brambles or a ditch and you go with them. I've tied Ken the plastic iguana to the handlebars so we both get a good view of the countryside.

I like lanes but I like main roads too sometimes, when I'm in the mood. That's because I like trains. Trains go where they want even more than lanes do, because they don't worry about ditches or hills or hedges. They go straight to wherever they're going, whatever's in the way. They're fast, and quite flat, which is clever when they travel through hilly places like Scotland without going up and down too much.

I like being a train when I'm on my bike on main roads. I wait for double white lines then Lars and I pedal in the middle of the road. Who wants to keep clattering into drains in the kerb and falling off? Not me.

I made trains this morning on Lars, a local train first with just a few carriages.

I went slow,

then very slow,

then even slower,

because that's what local trains do, they're never in a hurry. Like the bus to Minehead.

Then I turned into an express train with lots of carriages behind, stretching all the way back round the corner. There were hundreds of cars and lorries on the main road, so it didn't take long to put together a proper express train. By the end my train had fifty or sixty carriages, and I imagined Lars and I were the Royal Scot, racing to Edinburgh or Yorkshire.

Later, just before I stopped for Twix time I made a big goods train with ten vans, three lorries and two supermarket trailers. Goods trains go slower than passenger trains so I slowed right down to get it just right. It's important to be authentic. I hooted like a real train does, and all the cars and lorries hooted back and joined in. It was great fun. Then my camping stuff and special things fell off Lars's carrier when we were going down a hill. I put the brakes on hard and the whole train did an emergency stop.

No one helped me pick it all up.

Then we were back on the rails till we got to the station, which was a lay-by where I could stop and eat my Twix. Some of the passengers stuck their heads out and waved as they went by, just like they do in a real train. One van went by and bumped my bike and the driver leaned out and punched me. He bent Lars's handlebars too. Not very nice.

I like cows almost as much as I like trains. You see a lot of cows in the countryside because they like grass and the countryside is full of it.

Cows look at you when you stop to look at them over the gate.

What are they thinking when they look at you? Not that you're good to eat because they're vegetarian.

Do cows think? How should I know? When I look at them they stop eating and amble over to look at me more. Maybe they're short-sighted.

Amble, I like that word. I'll remember it in case I write a poem about cows.

Today the cows didn't stop eating for long, and they did lots of chewing while they watched me. I think it's Cud they're chewing, whatever that is. I did the same,

39

watching them while I chewed my Twix. Cows have got three or four stomachs that very cleverly turn grass into sloppy brown poo. Grass is tough and it often comes back up into their mouths for them to chew twice. I've only got one stomach so I don't think I've got a Cud, and I'd probably die or be very ill if I chewed grass. One stomach's enough for me, thank you.

Mum's meals often had lots of stringy greens like grass. She told me to eat them, son. And I did, because mums always want what's best for their children even if it does seem like the worst. When they got old mum and dad ate what are called Meals on Wheels, which was special hot food that was cold by the time they ate it.

Meals on Wheels. Another intriguing phrase. Dad tried to eat the plastic container once.

When I stopped to eat a cheese triangle and a Ryvita this afternoon a herd of cows ambled over and watched me. Cows don't have much to do except eat so they've got lots of time to amble. Not me, I'm too busy. We didn't say much and I got bored and they got bored, and they turned their backs on me and ate more grass. They had numbers tattooed in white on their backsides, and when they lined up it said 471322213416. Which was intriguing. I thought it might be a secret message or code, or a phone number. I stopped at the telephone box in the village and dialled it. It wasn't. I've written the number in my notebook.

Our family used to visit a lady down the road called Aunt Megs. She was very old and spent all day in bed and was fed through her tummy. She didn't have a tongue down there, just a hole and a tube, so I doubt if she could taste the difference between cabbage or trifle, or if it was breakfast or lunch. I held her hand last time, which was like an old oak twig.

Aunt Megs croaked like a frog and said You're lucky, young man, you've got your whole life ahead of you.

She was right. I still have my whole life ahead of me, though a bit less now than there was when she said it.

It was sad because Aunt Megs hadn't and she died a month later. We went to her funeral, and on her grave it said In Memory of Megs, a Faithful Friend. Which made her sound like her dog, Winston.

I bought more Twixes at a village post office. I ate one half waiting in the queue to pay because I was hungry, and the lady at the till couldn't Scan the Barcode because I'd split the wrapper. She kept getting the Barcode numbers wrong when she tapped them in. I said try the number on the cows' bottoms but that didn't work either. You never know.

It was getting dark so I put up my tent on some grass on the green outside the shop which was the same shape as my cheese triangles. Some boys kept pulling out the tent pegs. I didn't get much sleep.

I've got a dog. I didn't have one, now I have.

He runs up with a ball in his mouth and says Throw It in dog bark. He won't let go, which isn't very helpful. So I tug it and he growls and I growl back like I'm a dog. Which I'm not, but it's an Exercise in the Imagination.

He drops it and I throw it. It doesn't go far.

41

He runs to it, snaps it up and runs back with it. It's fun.

I tug and tug, he lets it go and I throw it again.
He runs to it, snaps it up and runs back with it.
I tug and tug, he lets it go and I throw it again.
He runs to it, snaps it up and runs back with it.
I tug and tug, he lets it go and I throw it again.
He runs to it, snaps it up and runs back with it.
I tug and tug, he lets it go and I throw it again.
He runs to it, snaps it up and runs back with it.
I tug and tug, he lets it go and I throw it again.
He runs to it, snaps it up and runs back with it.
I tug and tug, he lets it go and I throw it again.
He runs to it, snaps it up and runs back with it.
I tug and tug, he lets it go and I throw it again.

Maybe having a dog's not so much fun as I thought. I toss the ball into a bush. He hangs his head and looks puzzled. I bark and tell him I haven't got it and he grins. He barks again and says Throw it.

I tell him I haven't got it.

He barks and growls.

He's not clever, my dog, but it's no crisis.

What do I call him? Or her? Is he a boy or girl dog? Who cares, a dog's a dog.

What's your name, dog? I ask.

He won't say because dog's can't. There are millions of names for dogs and he must know his name but I'll never guess. I'll call him Kipper. He won't know a kipper's a dried up old fish.

I tell him, You're Kipper, my faithful friend, and he looks pleased and barks and grins and dribbles slobber.

Then he smells my below parts, which I haven't washed, but he doesn't seem to mind. Then he puts his paws on my shoulders and licks my face. His tongue's slimy like a snail.

Time to cycle on to Helen's. She must be getting very worried about her hamster book.

Kipper runs alongside Lars. I ring my bell and he barks and I bark back and I ring my bell again. We're both very happy. We get to a wood and stop and I tiptoe in. That's what woods make you do, you slow down and move like a mouse. I stand under a tree and think Green.

It's quiet. Nothing moves apart from an old brown leaf dancing on a twig. Is it happy? How should I know? Maybe it knows something about the Life Beyond we don't. I'm writing a poem.

A brown leaf dancing
Are you dead or just dying?
Or are you doing what they call the Dance of Death?

A bit short but it's a start.

I can hear people talking. I creep closer and listen.

Has it got crown fathers raised and emarginations on the outer web level with tertial tip?

Check, he's got those.

And a fairly short, square-ended tail, and indistinct yellow-white supercilium?

Yep, them too.

Pale edges to tertials and secondaries?

Yep.

And pale eye ring?

Yep.

That's it. Got him nailed.

Where's Kipper?

I look around. Where's my faithful friend gone?

Kipper, I shout. Kipper!

A tree smacks me in the chest.

Piss off you fucking idiot!

A talking tree's hit me.

It's not a talking tree it's a green man. And there's another. They're green all over. Green coats, green hats, green trousers, green boots, green binoculars, green telescopes.

Where's Friar Tuck? I ask and laugh.

They don't, which is curious.

One Green Man says That was an icterine you scared away. He points up at the trees.

I look through his telescope and see Green, lots of it.

Icky what? I ask.

An icterine, arsehole.

I look through the telescope again. I can't see an Icky, unless Icky's a green blob.

Green's calming. I've already forgotten the Icky. I'm experiencing Eternal Peace. It's restful, like being on Sally's sofa listening to her Japanese music.

But what's that? Through the telescope there's a green blob moving. It's a tiny green hopping bird.

Is that Icky? I ask. The green blob?

That green blob's a bloody Icterine Warbler, they say, and look very angry.

You've disturbed it, you little turd, and it's very rare.

How do you know it's rare? I ask. There could be Ickys

all over the place. You can't be everywhere at the same time.

We're birders, they say, and nod smugly.

Does Icky know it's rare?

What do you mean? They look puzzled.

Does Icky know it's rare? They look more puzzled.

Does any bird know it's rare? I ask. And would it care?

Look, chum, just piss off. We don't want it disturbed. We're hoping it'll breed if it's left in peace.

Propagating's something I know about, I worked at the garden centre. These men need advice. I tell them I think you should know Icky can't breed on its own, it needs to find a girl Ickorette. If Ickys are rare that could be difficult.

One of the men gets out a camera. Sod it, I'll take a pic of him and get it up on the website. And we'll tick it off on the species list and move on.

Where should Icky be? I ask.

Nowhere near here. Eastern Europe somewhere, the Balkans, Crimea.

Aren't you worried about him?

Worried? What do you mean?

Icky's lost. He's on his own. He'll never find an Ickorette here to propagate with. Shouldn't you catch him and send him in a parcel to where he should be?

They look at me as if I am mad.

We're off. A Pectoral sandpiper's been spotted. Be a first for us.

I look through the telescope again.

There's Kipper, I shout.

Kipper?

My faithful friend.

Kipper's leaping around in the green barking, and lifting his leg on tree stumps.

Where's Icky now? He's nowhere, Icky's gone.

Icky's rarer still now, I tell them. One of the green men raises his fist but I'm on Lars pedalling away fast.

The green men didn't care about poor Icky.

Icky's lost
Tired and sad
He's miles from home
And all alone

It rhymes. My best so far.

I cycle on thinking Green Thoughts.

Green looks better than it tastes. I hid mum's greens in a handkerchief once when she wasn't looking and just ate the chops and potato.

Then I remember Kipper. He's not running beside me. Like Icky he's gone too. I had a dog and now I don't. He wasn't my faithful friend for very long.

I've started another poem.

Do Ickys care
If they're rare?

A bit short.

I'm in a pub drinking beer. I asked for mango squash

when I went to the pub with Sally and Bernhard, and Bernhard told me it's not a man's drink and if you ask for one in a pub they'll throw you out. I didn't think I'd like beer, but I'm enjoying the second pint more than the first.

The pub's empty except for a man in the corner looking at his phone. He's tapping numbers in.

Bernhard told me about mobile phones before he left Sally. He wanted to sell me his old one but Sally told him I didn't have what they call a Signal at the hut. But Bernhard still tried to make me buy it and Sally got cross and said she'd Withhold her Favours, whatever they are, if he carried on. Favours must be important because Bernhard looked very worried.

Bernhard said mobile phones send pictures too. He tapped a few buttons on his phone and showed me some photos of ladies' bottoms and bosoms. And a rude down below part with a beard. Guess who posed for these? he said, and smirked at Sally. Sure you don't want to buy it?

Sally hit him because I think he must have been what's called Two Timing her.

Bernhard said we're all bathing in a sea of Electromagnetic Waves. They zap everywhere at the speed of light arriving before they leave. Bernhard said there are more mobile phones than people on this planet. All the phone numbers lined up would stretch to Australia, longer even than the numbers of all the cows if they lined up their bottoms.

Sally and Bernhard call mobile phones Mobiles. Like car boot sales are called Boots. Bernhard said if I bought his mobile my voice would zap off to a tall mast somewhere, then to another mast somewhere else, then to another, then another, then zap all the way down to the exact phone I want it to. Which would be Sally's.

Sally doesn't just talk, she sends words through her phone. Bernhard said it's called Texting. Sally types words she wants to say into her phone and they zap to masts and then you read them on your phone wherever you are.

What's the point? I want to talk to Sally not write words to her then her write words to me.

Mobile signals go through walls, they're powerful. More powerful than electric drills which go through walls but take much longer and make builders drink lots of tea and eat too many chocolate biscuits.

I'd like Sally to send me a picture of herself but she can't because I haven't got a mobile. I'll buy one tomorrow. Then I'll send Sally a picture of me on my way to give Helen back her hamster book.

Helen will be pleased, she must be very worried.

Is it my voice Sally hears if I phone her? I don't think it is, I think it's Electricity. Bernhard said mobiles send your voice in Packets to the mast. Packets of what? Not like sugar snapcrackle packets because they're cardboard. I don't really care as I want to hear Sally's voice even if it is packets of Electricity. If it sounds like Sally it's no crisis.

Dad made phones out of baked bean tins and a piece of string in the garden.

He'd say Can you hear me, son? Over.

I'd say Yes, dad. Over.

It got boring because I could see dad all the time and he could see me, so we knew we could hear each other anyway without the baked bean tins.

I'm buying a mobile. I'm in Taunton which is a big town. I don't know which phone shop to choose as they all look the same with very unfriendly faces. I choose one with no customers.

Good morning, sir, says the man. His hair sticks up like a hedgehog and he's got tight trousers like ladies' tights.

I need a mobile. I want to talk to Sally, I tell him. I'm cycling to Budleigh Salterton to return Helen's book.

No problem, sir, he says, we've a terrific selection second to none. Look at this beauty, the HK732. If you're cycling it tells you how fast you're going. It's a fitness tool, too, and tells you how many times you pedal a minute, your heart rate, and where you're going by utilising the inbuilt compass and directional maps. And you can play games and set personal performance goals.

But will it let me talk to Sally? I ask.

Of course. How often do you want to talk to her?

All the time, I say. I like Sally.

You'll need a contract then, sir. Unlimited texts and three gigabytes of storage and internet usage, plus this special prestige imitation leather red case. All yours for a once only exclusive deal of just £47 a month. A snip.

Whooooh. That's most of my benefit payment, I'm shocked.

It all depends how much you like Sally, doesn't it, sir?

I like her very much, I say.

Or, he says, you could pay as you go, but I wouldn't recommend it.

An intriguing phrase, Pay as you Go. I can't Pay as I Go especially when I'm on Lars as I'd fall off and get run over by a lorry. And if it happened while I was phoning

Sally she'd hear me getting injured or killed, which would upset her. I'll go for the contract, I say.

The right decision, sir.

He shakes my hand. It's reassuring to speak to professionals.

I've got a mobile.

The salesman told me I'd bought a mobile, but it's got a plug and a wire. Sally's hadn't. When I switch it on it doesn't work. I can't plug it in inside my tent or on my bike. I'd go back to the phone shop but it's late and I want to pitch my tent.

I'm on a campsite which is full of tents bigger than my hut. They've got kitchens and TVs and freezers and tables and chairs and blow up sofas.

A boy watches me fiddling with my mobile. He says Give it here and does a lot of tapping. It's not charged, he says and runs off.

I talk to the lady in the camp office and she says You need to plug it in for a few hours to charge it, but the office is shut at night. You'll have to plug it in the toilet sockets.

I pitch my tent outside the men's toilets. Which are not very nice. They smell and they're dirty, but it's no crisis. Men don't point their bottoms down. Mum taught me to point my bottom down which is why I never need to do any scouring with Brillo.

I'll have to watch my mobile charging in case someone steals it. I stick toilet paper up my nose and hold my breath every time I go in to check it's still there charging.

I cook myself beans on toast on my camping gas. I leave my plate to soak before I wash it. When I was young

I helped mum do the washing up. I'd scrape at hard bits on the pans but never got them squeaky clean enough for mum. She'd say Not good enough, son, best to leave plates and pans to soak, the hot water softens the hard bits.

A lot of my wisdom about life comes from mum's advice.

Every time someone goes in the toilets I go in too. If they're doing a number two I wait and stuff toilet paper in my ears as well as up my nose. I don't like listening to squelches. Three youths go in to pee and I watch them.

What are you staring at, shithead? they say. They shout and call me Pervert. One of them holds his willy out and says Want to suck it, you little creep?

I don't think so, I'm too busy watching my mobile charging, I tell them. They hit me and bruise my lip.

I didn't get much sleep, so a lot of campers must have bladder problems. I watched all of them go in and come out just in case. But my mobile's charged because a green light's come on and green means Go. It does at traffic lights so it must be the same with mobiles.

The boy comes back as I'm eating my sugar snapcrackles. He saw me fiddling with my mobile again. I tell him I don't know how to phone Sally.

Give it here, he says. Now swipe it.

He shows me how to swipe and then phone Sally, but she's not in. He says Send her some words instead.

Which I do.

I say Hi Sally. I'm fine. How are you? Over.

It took me a very long time as I only used one finger

and the mobile kept typing in things it thought I wanted to say but that I definitely didn't want to say. It was maddening.

It's predictive, the boy told me.

I look up Predictive in my dictionary. It says Generating letters or words a user is likely to enter next on the basis of those that have already been entered.

But I hadn't entered any before as it was my first text, so how did it know what I might have entered already when there was no before for me to have entered any? Not very intelligent.

Sally's sent me back some words and letters. She says Who r u. Over what?

Which is curious because Sally knows me very well.

I'm washing my plate and mug. I miss having a lot of washing up to do, but I like living alone and doing exactly what I like when I like. That's why my life is so rich compared to other people's.

At mum and dad's the draining board was always full of dirty knives and forks and plates and mugs and pans after dinner. Mum used three saucepans, a frying pan and two mixing bowls for cooking, even when she was making scrambled eggs. I'd sort all the dirties into sizes for her and make piles. I'd put a small pan into a bigger pan and a bigger pan into an even bigger pan. I'd put all the knives in the washing water together and line them all up pointing the same way. Then the spoons and the forks and the teaspoons. I'd wash everything up one by one, leaving plates in the soapy water so the hard bits went soft first. It's important to do things properly.

In the hut I only had to wash up one knife and fork, one mug, one plate and one pan. Not really much to do, so I couldn't make piles. So sometimes I'd use three knives and forks and put a fish finger on one plate and a fish finger on another and one on another and one on another, and drink my mango squash in three mugs, one at a time. Then I imagined there was more to wash up. Which there was.

Some boys laughed at my tent, which was dad's when he was in the scouts. It's very old. They said it was the colour of shit and wrinkled like an old man's willy. Their dads came over and smacked them.

I'm shopping at a supermarket. It's where you get bargains, Sally says.

At the door a lady says Give me a pound, you can have this trolley.

A bargain already and I haven't even gone inside. I see why people shop at supermarkets. I'll tow the trolley behind Lars, there's room in it for my tent and sleeping bag.

Time to look for bargains. The supermarket's packed and everyone's filling their trolleys. There are my sugar snapcrackles in what they call a Family Pack. A wobbly sign says Two for One. I think this means I buy one packet and I get another free. I buy two packs and get four. You can't have too many sugar snapcrackles. I haven't got a family now that mum and dad are in a home, but I like sugar snapcrackles so I'll imagine I'm a family and eat two breakfasts. Why not?

Where are the fish fingers?

53

A lady in a uniform asks me what I'm looking for.

Fish fingers and bargains, I tell her.

Plenty of those, sir, she says and smiles. Aisle number seven for fish fingers, in the frozen cabinets past the sauces half way along.

Aisle. An intriguing word.

I go up and down, up and down, up and down. Past magazines, televisions, toilet rolls, soups, pickles, coffee, scouring pads, and find the fish fingers at last. When I open the glass door Jack Frost jumps out. It's cold. They're Buy One Get One Free. I buy three and get six. This supermarket's better than the pound shop.

I'm grabbing bargain after bargain and dropping them in my trolley. Pea and brie farmhouse soups, Aunt Bessie's mega dumplings, twinpot choco sponges, pork faggots, turkey and chilli dippers, frazzle snacklets, cheesy chipsticks, munch bunches, Star Wars blast off yoghurts, meerkat puffs. My trolley's bursting, I'd like to live here.

What now?

A lady in a uniform smiles at my bulging trolley and says Do you have a loyalty card, sir? It could be worth your while. It entitles you to a range of special rewards and benefits. Your favourite brands at extra reduced prices, offers tailored to your needs, Christmas savers, coupons for our baby club, offers on the go, balloon flights, vouchers for skin softeners for your wife or partner. The more you buy the more points you're awarded. It's the perfect way to save on that all-important household budget. And you can monitor your balance on your mobile and watch it grow on your own online club account where you can swap household tips with club colleagues.

Why not? I sign up. Monitoring my balance on my mobile sounds intriguing.

Let's get your trolley scanned first, the lady says. We'll use the self-service checkout. She picks my bargains out of the trolley one by one and points them at a machine which makes pip pip noises. At last it's empty.

Right, sir, she says. Your card, please.

I'm paying cash, I tell her, and hand her all the money in my pocket.

She counts it and says Only twelve pounds here, sir, your cart comes to ninety-seven and forty six pence. We'll need your card and pin.

She pushes my card into a slot and says Tap your pin in now, sir.

I've forgotten the number. It's dad's birthday a month and a bit before or after but I can't remember which, and I can't remember dad's birthday either, which is curious seeing as he's had so many. I can remember mine, which is curious too, because I'm much younger and had a lot fewer.

Let's stop and think shall we, sir, she says.

We stop and think. I think of one number, then another, then another, and she taps them in one at a time and says Sorry, Sorry, Sorry.

The machine says No to them all.

We'll do a reset, she says.

The machine makes noises like Sally's Japanese music and lights flash.

I think hard and have an idea. She taps in the long number made by the cows' bottoms but that doesn't work either.

I think even harder and at last remember my Pin. She taps the numbers in and a green light flashes and all the bargains are mine.

Right, where's your car, sir? she says. You'll need help to load.

I'm on Lars, I say. I'm cycling to Helen's to give her back her book.

She looks puzzled. Wait here, she says, I'll call my supervisor, and talks into her mobile.

No car, sir? says the supervisor when she comes up. How do you intend to get all this shopping home?

I'll tow it on the trolley, I explain. I'm cycling to Helen's to give her back her book.

The trolley belongs to the supermarket, sir.

I don't think so, I say. I bought it from a lady outside. I paid a pound.

They look cross.

I'm calling the manager, the supervisor says.

A man with spiky hair and tight trousers like ladies' leggings comes over.

I think we have a problem, sir. What we're going to do is empty your trolley and refund your money.

But what about my sugar snapcrackles and fish fingers and all the other bargains?

You should have thought of that.

Dad told me Son, it's important to stand up for your rights. I tell them I think you've forgotten that the customer is always right.

A fat security man grabs my arm and pushes me back outside to Lars.

And don't come back, you little scumbag, he says.

Not very nice. It doesn't happen in pound shops.

I'm worried about Sally. She was sad not to get the new job she went for and I think I know why. She can't spell. I found more words from her in my mobile. She said UNCTRTN who u r. W@ U W.

You have to know how to spell to get a job these days. So I've been thinking hard about not going to Helen's to return her book but going to Sally's to teach her to spell so she can get a new job.

I've thought harder still and I think I'm going to Helen's first, as she must be needing her book badly by now. I won't send Sally any more words if she can't read them. But I'll go to Sally's straight after.

Sally cried when she didn't get her new job. Everyone cries sometimes. I don't. Life must be sad for most people. I don't feel sad very often, and if I do it's about Sally and how much I wish I was with her. I took a packet of jammy dodgers to her house after Bernhard left her and it made her cry. I ate most of them because she was crying and didn't feel hungry. I told her a joke and she cried even more, but it was no crisis.

Poor Sally.

I'm cycling to Helen's again. All the road signs we pass are for cars. One says the speed limit's forty not sixty and I ignore it, because Lars and me don't go that fast, even when we're in a hurry. Which we're not.

At last. Here's a sign meant for me. THINK BIKE.
I stop. I close my eyes and think hard.
I'm thinking BIKE about

Lars's handlebars
His wheel nuts
His chain
His saddle my bottom's sitting on
His spokes, one of which is broke
His handlebars
His gears
His brakes
His bell

I'm feeling calm like Zen monks.

If they THINK BIKE they can cycle miles without leaving their room. They don't get very fit but they do find Universal Peace, which is more important than a six pack in this troubled world.

I'm dozing, my head's bulging with Universal Peace. A lorry with a skip races by and blows me off Lars and we land in a ditch. Lars isn't damaged but my Universal Peace is.

Skip, an intriguing word. I look it up in my dictionary. It says To Jump Lightly over a Rope. Or to Leave One Place Quickly to Go to Another. Or to Not Do Something you Should Do. Or A Large Metal Container to Put Unwanted Objects in.

Skip's a word to use very carefully, otherwise what you want to happen might not happen and something you don't will.

I'm drinking beer in another pub. I'm achieving Universal Peace even more quickly with beer than THINKING BIKE.

Men at the bar in yellow jackets are getting calm with beer and reading newspapers. They've got yellow jackets on. I think they're mending the road. I'd like a yellow jacket as it would make me shine bright as the sun and lorries could see me on Lars and not knock me off. The men are rolling cigarettes and reading the paper and saying Manu's strikers are rubbish. Manu must have lent them his matches. He's probably Spanish and having a siesta somewhere.

I'm cycling to Helen's again.

Which sounds as if I've been to Helen's already, but I haven't, this is the first time.

I try hard to say what I mean but words don't always mean what I mean them to. Maybe I should have said I'm cycling again to Helen's. But that sounds as if I've been walking or running or swimming to Helen's. I don't think having a dictionary is enough if I'm going to be a Student of the English language.

This afternoon I had a cycling friend. My shadow biked alongside Lars and me for hours then got stuck behind when we put on a spurt before Twix time. When I got back on Lars he wasn't there at all because it was cloudy.

Shadows like sun. Very much. The sunnier it is the darker they are. The sun today made Lars and me very light and our shadows very dark. When it's sunny it's impossible for me to catch up with my shadow, and if I'm going the other way my shadow can't catch up with me. Shadows always chase you or run away from you.

I can't see any what are called Distinguishing Features

in my shadow like my hair or eyes or clothes, only my shape. It's what's called a Silhouette. I looked Silhouette up in my dictionary and it says it's The Dark Shape of Something or Someone in Restricted Light against a Brighter Background.

Sometimes I need a dictionary for my dictionary.

Everyone's shadow looks the same. Elton John's would look like mine if he was cycling to Helen's. A bit fatter.

My feet are hot pedalling to Helen's. It's Twix time. I'm looking at grass bumps in the field. They're called Barrows and primitive men are buried in them. Some people say ghosts of these primitive dead men come out at night like bats and badgers. When we went to Stonehenge Uncle Jeff told me dead men come out of holes in barrows in the dark and go back down them when it's light. It was the last story he told me because just afterwards he went down a hole himself in the churchyard.

If dead men in barrows do come alive again as ghosts they probably run round waving swords and rattling chains and fighting each other, because that's what people did in primitive times, even polite gentle ones. There probably wasn't much else to do.

Rumble noises up the lane. Black smoke. Maybe it's a tank with invading armies. Wars start at any time, even when people are cycling or sitting on the toilet. Whatever it is here it comes. It's a motorbike and sidecar, and it's skidding all over the lane and it's black and old and rattling. It bumps up on the grass and I have to jump out of the way to stop getting squashed.

The rider's got goggles on like pilots in the War. Dad

60

likes wars. Not fighting in them, just watching them in Spitfire films, it's safer.

The man takes off his helmet and says I know you.

I know you too, I say. You're the man with the red and green flags who was too busy to see me and who said the meat display in the shop looked like a Polish film. And you've got a limp on the other leg from mine. I'm cycling to Helen's to return her book.

See those barrows? he says. Have they moved? I'm Hardaker the Conceptualist. I'm studying the displacement of static prehistoric structures and their random redistribution. Those tumuli are repositories of cremations from bronze age funerary rites. I'm working on a site-specific installation for a Frankfurt gallery, a series of conceptual artworks derived from statistical modelling and relational databases.

I get out my dictionary but he hasn't stopped talking and already there are far too many words to look up.

They're bronze age mounds, he says. I've waited years to watch them move.

This man's odd, but some people are. I said this to Sally and Bernhard once and Bernhard laughed and said You really do take the biscuit.

Which I did. The last jammy dodger.

Wheelbarrows move, I tell Mr Hardaker. But you have to push them like I did at the garden centre. I think it's quite a good joke but he doesn't laugh because he's rabbiting on saying I've access to unique aerial photography plus an SMR dump of spatial GPS geographic data.

We sit in the hedge for an hour and watch the grass bumps not moving. His jacket smells of fungus.

I'm getting bored. I like activity.

Stop fidgeting, Mr Hardaker pokes me in the stomach. And don't stare at them. Look out of the corner of your eye so they don't see us watching.

After another whole day which is really only half an hour I'm very bored. And I've got a neck crick. I tell Mr Hardaker my life's too busy to sit watching barrows not moving. I need to get to Helen's to return her book, she must be frantic with worry. They're not going to move, I tell him.

They will, he says. They're governed by a universal law positing the necessity of random displacement manifested across time.

This man sounds very clever, but so did Bernhard, and he wasn't.

Patience, Mr Hardaker says. If we wait long enough they'll skip across the field like spring lambs.

They don't. We wait. Another whole day. Other people's lives are dull.

A bramble tickles my nose and I sneeze. My stomach's rumbling and Mr Hardaker looks cross. My knees are numb and I tell him I've got to get up or I won't be able to cycle to Helen's.

He says You're clearly embarked on an objective of similarly pressing merit to mine. If we could only accelerate the inevitable. To be frank, I'm facing a fiscal crisis, my grant funding runs out in three weeks. Come on, let's call on Rawson. Leave your bike in the ditch.

Can I wear your goggles? I ask him.

I'm in the sidecar wearing goggles. Everything's orange, even the sky which is actually blue. I'm in that crackly film I watched with dad. I'm a gunner in a Spitfire and I'm shooting at everything, yatta bang. We're on fire, the ejector seat's jammed, and I keep pressing switches but nothing's working.

Lean at the corners, Mr Hardaker's shouts. I'm leaning. I shimmy to the left, shimmy to the right, like mum and dad at the British Legion dance.

I've fallen out, bumped my head, grazed my knee, bruised my nose and torn my trousers, but it's no crisis.

Come on, come on, get back in, no time to lose, says Mr Hardaker. And we race off, me choking on black smoke.

Mr Rawson was out. I walked miles back to Lars. Mr Hardaker said he had urgent business in the opposite direction.

A dog went by in a car and stuck his head out of the window and barked This way to Helen's. How did he know where I was going? Maybe animals have a sixth sense. Or a seventh.

I've stopped in a lay-by. A fat man and a lady are sunbathing outside their camper van. The man's snoring. The sun's burned them red all over like lobsters. I creep closer, but it's not sunburn, it's ants. There are ants all over them. It's important to help people in times of trouble, so I grab a branch to brush them off and give the man a slap.

What the ...! He opens his eyes and raises his fists.

It's not ants it's tattoos. It's rude to stare, but I do. Their tattoos are like doodles I did in my school colouring book. Ink shapes, flowers and anchors and swords.

The lady's got a heart tattooed over her real heart, and bracelets round her wrists and hoops round her ankles.

You're staring at our tattoos, the man says.

Why not? I tell him. Tattoos are meant to be looked at. Otherwise, what's the point? You can't not look at something when it's shouting Look at Me.

The lady's wearing a brassiere. I try hard not to look at her bosoms. She sits up and I'm shocked, her brassiere's a tattoo too.

It takes all sorts.

The man's got words tattooed on his arm saying Pam, my one true love as long as I live. And a picture of a lady. The lady has a picture of a man on her shoulder saying George I belong to you till death us do part.

You like them? says the man, pointing at his chest.

I don't think so, I'm thinking. I wouldn't want ink doodles all over me.

But be polite when you meet new people, son, dad told me.

How do you do, George and Pam. Your tattoos are intriguing, I tell them. George and Pam look at each other.

Actually, he says, I'm Vic and this is Elaine. We've just married. We're on our honeymoon.

But your tattoo says Pam's your one true love, Vic. And your tattoo says you'll love George till death do you part, Elaine.

We're both divorced, they say. We haven't got the old tattoos removed yet, says Elaine, pointing at George. Vic jabs Pam on his chest and says That deceiving bitch is my ex-wife. He bares his teeth like the dog that tore my trousers in the park.

I can see why he divorced Pam, she's got a beard like Uncle Gilbert's but it could be where the ink ran.

Don't upset yourself, love, says Elaine, and holds his hand. We're getting new tattoos done of the two of us.

Would you like a tattoo? Vic asks.

Who do you love, young man? asks Elaine.

I don't have to think hard. I love Sally, I say.

I could do you a tattoo of her, Vic says. I've a drill and inks in the van.

Why not? Sally would be with me all the time.

Where do you want it? Vic asks. Back, front, arm, leg?

I think hard again. I won't see Sally if she's on my back. I'd like her on my tummy.

No worries, says Vic. Tell me what Sally looks like. I give him my secret picture. It's one of the ones Sally took in the booth outside Tesco. She didn't like it and threw it in the bin and I took it out and put in my pocket when she wasn't looking. You can't see her nose where it's creased. We go inside the camper van which smells of gas. There's what's left of a Full English Breakfast on a plate.

Vic wipes my stomach with a wipe and gets ink bottles out of a cupboard like dad used for his fountain pen. He snaps rubber gloves on like a doctor's and points his drill at my stomach. It buzzes like a dentist's, and I wince, but it's no crisis. It's scratchy and tickly being tattooed, and when it hurts I fidget and Vic says KEEP STILL.

Poets like Wordworth say You must suffer for love, and I will. For Sally.

Do you want Sally nude? asks Vic.

I think hard.

Don't worry, says Vic, leave it to me. I'm sure Sally's

got a lovely body. She looks great in her passport picture. Right, stay still, I'm starting on her chin, he says.

It takes ages.
Now her eye.
It takes more ages.
Now her other eye.
It must be tomorrow by now.
STAY STILL, I'm doing Sally's mouth and lips.
And now her hair.
KEEP STILL.

Don't forget Sally's nose, I tell him. She's got one, but in the photo it's just a crease.

Would you like some loving words like we've got? Elaine asks. Vic can tattoo Sally, Love you forever, if you like.

Why not?

After MORE hours of bzzzzing Vic turns his drill off. There, finished, have a look.

I bend down and look.

Where's Sally? I can't see her.

It's because you're creasing your stomach, says Elaine. Keep it straight and bend your neck. She looks wonderful, doesn't she?

I look again.

I don't think so, I say. Sally's upside down.

Not to us. Have another look. Elaine holds up a mirror.

That's not Sally, I say, it's someone else!

Vic and Elaine look at the photo and say No it's not.

It's not Sally, it's Aunt Megs! And she's naked and all shrivelled up!

Not from here she isn't, says Elaine. She's got a lovely young woman's body. Like mine was once.

I don't think so, Elaine, I'm thinking.

It's not Sally, I keep telling them. Sally doesn't look like a dried up old prune.

You're creasing your stomach up and seeing her upside down. She looks lovely from here.

I don't often get what they call Perturbed. But if Sally washes my shirt like she did for Bernhard when he wasn't wearing his trousers she'll see my tattoo and think I love someone else and get jealous, even if it is actually Aunt Megs. I would if Sally had a tattoo of someone else and not me on her stomach.

Can you untattoo Aunt Megs?

Tattoos are forever, sweetheart, Elaine says. Unless you have surgery to remove them. Look, don't worry, Sally will look like that in years to come when she's older. That's the beauty of tattoos, they express eternal love and devotion.

Vic looks very cross. Look, chum, what do you expect for nothing, Leonardo da bloody Vinci? And you kept fidgeting.

He pushes me outside and slams the door.

I ride off towards Helen's. It's lucky Aunt Megs is dead and won't see my tattoo of her nude and think I'm in love with her forever. It's no crisis.

I've left my bicycle clips in Vic and Elaine's camper van so I'm tucking my trouser bottoms into my socks. I've got short legs. I know this because when I buy trousers I have to turn the bottoms up. But I've got a limp so one leg looks better turned up two and a bit folds and the other three folds.

I use sellotape for turning up trouser bottoms but Sally turned up my new pair using stitches. They're my favourites. She uses invisible stitches and I have to use my microscope to see them.

Sally made me stand in my pants in the kitchen with the door closed while she did the sewing. Which was probably best, because I think things happen between men and women when they've got their trousers and skirts off.

Dad's old trousers have turn ups, though he wears jogging bottoms in the Home and the nurses have to stretch the elastic round his waist, which is a long way and getting longer. But dad's are turn-out turn ups. You can see the turn ups on the outside, which is old-fashioned. But so's dad. My trouser legs have turn-in turn ups, which is very modern. I call mine turnips. When I got my new trousers I said to Sally Could you sew my turnips up for me? And we laughed. I like making Sally laugh, it's good for her Health and Wellbeing.

I'm cycling with the wind in my hair. I'm enjoying it while I can as when I'm bald I won't be able to.

My bus ticket to Minehead is in my pocket. It reminds me how important it is to go straight to wherever you're going, not like the bus to Minehead that wriggled all over the place and went everywhere else first. I need to get to Helen's, and quick. She needs her book.

My pockets are bulging with important stuff. A lot from Christmas crackers. I fiddle with it all when I entertain Sally. I pull things out like lucky dip and say

What have we here?

That's what magicians say when they pull things out of a hat, even though they know exactly what they have here.

I pull out a pack of tiny playing cards, then a magnifying glass, then a trumpet, then a hair slide (which I'm saving for Sally), then a pair of plastic red lips, then a moustache. I try not to pull the same thing out twice because it's not so entertaining. You learn with experience.

I'd like a bird's nest in my pocket as part of my act. It would look like ordinary bulgings to the audience till a bird flew out to catch flies then flew back in to feed its chicks. And the chicks would make small trouser bulges and cheeping noises and get bigger as they got fatter then waggle their wings and fly out. It would make a very intriguing entertainment.

I've been thinking hard and I'd prefer a blue tit's nest in my pocket, not a bird like a buzzard's. A buzzard's chicks would grow too big and burst the seams and peck holes in my trousers and Sally would have to keep sewing them up.

I've noticed that young people have holes in their jeans and flappy splits at the knees. Their families must be very poor, and it's a sad reflection on the state of the world today that a decent pair of trousers is beyond the family budget. And clothes are cheaper today than they were in the past. They're made in what are called Sweat Shops in China by tiny children using even tinier stitches than Sally's who are paid in bowls of rice.

Mum bought my school trousers from the shop in the high street called Brambles the Outfitters. She'd say

Let's go and fit you out, son. And we did. Mr Bramble measured my inside leg which felt a bit rude, then gave me trousers much too big because mum wanted them to last. What was the point of measuring?

I've got marbles in my pockets and I roll them between my fingers and they squeak like chirpy birds when they rub together. I've been planning my act and I don't think I'd need a real bird's nest in my pocket at all when I'm entertaining. I'd just twiddle the marbles and make out it's blue tits. Magicians call that an Illusion. Illusions are important when you're a Man of Mystery like I want to be.

If I had trousers with pockets all the way down the legs like a chest of drawers I could have blue tits, blackbirds, wagtails and lots of other birds nesting in them. I'd make out I was a tree, and wave my arms and drop sweet wrappers like autumn leaves.

You need to plan your act carefully when you want to be a professional entertainer. Otherwise you get booed and don't get asked back. I'd rehearse cracker jokes I'd keep in an elastic band in my pocket before I went on, and wear a fake moustache and beard. The moustache and beard are important, because people need to know I'm a professional entertainer in costume and not just a bore like Uncle Nigel who tells jokes all the time, even when he's asleep.

I tried out my cracker jokes on Billy, Nils and Nita. I don't think Nils got his. I said What's got four legs but can't walk, Nils? I couldn't tell if he was thinking, you can't with chairs. And he is Swedish. I gave him ten minutes just in case then told him. What's got four legs but can't walk, Nils? A table! I laughed but Nils didn't.

Different things must be funny in Sweden so I probably won't go on tour there.

The answer's also a chair when I think about it, so maybe he felt insulted.

My favourite cracker joke is Who hides in the oven at Christmas? A mince spy. I'll have to make sure I don't laugh when I tell it, which will be difficult, comedians don't.

Sometimes when I entertain Sally I fill my plastic water pistol with mango squash and squirt it in my mouth. You're dead, I say and fall over. Sally laughs, and I laugh too.

I'm resting by a hedge in a field having a Thinking Day.

I haven't measured anything for ages. There are sticks in the hedge but they're different lengths and they'd all measure things differently. If I told someone how much something measured using a stick they'd have to have one the same length to tell.

Measuring things in the country is difficult because everything's big. Fields, trees, hedges, hills, rivers. How could I measure this field with a stick? Farmers wouldn't use one, a stick's much too small. They measure in acres. An acre's big. You can't see an acre, it's a huge lump of grass or corn that disappears over a hill where you can't see the rest of it to measure. Farmer's probably measure their fields in cows and sheep as well as in acres. They'd say This is a five cow field. Or if they were a sheep farmer they'd say This is a ten sheep field. Much easier. There are lots of ways to measure the world and you can't have too many.

If I had still had my faithful friend, which I did till he ran off, I could measure this field by the number of throws of a ball it takes to get to the end. It would be easy because my dog would do all the running and bring the ball back to me each time. I'd only have to walk on to where he dropped the ball and then pick it up and throw it again and sit down and eat my Twix till he got back. It would be an Efficient Use of Available Resources.

But I haven't got a dog now and I haven't got a field to measure, so I won't bother, I'll just have a quiet Thinking Day.

My Thinking Day is not as relaxing as I'd hoped. It's made me think that with all my talents I could be helping sad and unhappy people.

It's good making people laugh as an entertainer, but when my act's finished they have to go back home to their sad lives.

Maybe I could be a Psychiatrist, and help people make perfect lives for themselves like mine. Being a Psychiatrist's quite easy. Mum and dad sent me to one and she just sat in her chair for a whole hour asking me questions like What do you think you should do? How does that make you feel? Is that what you think?

I got cross and told her mum and dad were paying for answers not questions and didn't have money to waste.

I asked her What do you think? How do you feel? and she just growled and bit her nails and kept looking at her watch. I told her that people who bite their nails are unhappy, and I think you, madam, need a Psychiatrist more than me. She growled some more and said Time's up. So I left. I don't think she was very good at her job.

If I was a Psychiatrist I'd give sad people all the benefits of my wisdom and loads of advice. Otherwise, what's the point?

I suppose I could be a philosopher. Philosophers ask important questions about the world and about how to be a good human being.

I've looked up Philosopher in my dictionary. It's made up of two bits. Philo means Love Of and Sophia means Wisdom. But philosopher's spend all their time asking questions. And when they think they've found an answer another philosopher will say No you Haven't, and ask another question. They have to keep asking questions in a way, because if they found an answer to everything they could all agree with they wouldn't have careers any more and they'd have to get jobs delivering parcels or plumbing. Philosophers make people more confused than they were before, so being one must be very unsatisfactory. If I was a philosopher asking questions like Where does the universe end? I'd just sit round thinking about it, which would not be very helpful. It would be far better to be a spaceman and shoot off in a rocket to the end of the universe and actually find out. It's like when I wanted to know where the combe ends. Asking Billy, Nils and Nita didn't help, because how could they know? I kept walking till I got to the end and found out.

On a Thinking Day I often wonder who the I that I am is. Sometimes I think there must be two me's. If I ask myself a question and answer it, it's as if I'm talking to someone else. I say You should do this, You should do that. Or one of us says it. But who am I actually talking to? And who's doing the answering?

Is there another Me?

One Me must be wiser than the other Me to be giving the answer. Who is the Me that's the cleverer one? How should I know. How should either of us.

The Me who says You do that, You do this, is always very bossy. Just like dad was when he said Clean your teeth, son, NOW.

I've good teeth thanks to dad, a bit yellow. Dad hasn't got any now, so he probably didn't take his own advice.

I've been thinking hard, and that's what's so important about having Thinking Days. I've had what's called a Eureka Moment like Archie Medes. This is why I buy Twixes – there's one for me and one for him. I'm feeding the inner man as well the outer one. I'm just as excited as he was, but I'm not going to run all the way home without any clothes on like he did.

I'm wet through, it's been raining and I've been cycling fast to get to Helen's to return her book. I've skidded on a drain and fallen in a ditch. Another spoke's broke and Lars is lying on top of me. Ken the iguana broke his tail, but it's no crisis, iguanas grow a new one. But Ken's plastic so it's unlikely.

Because of the crash I've got a headache and a pain in my knee.

Time for some pills. I've got Paracetemols in my bag, so I'll take two.

It's intriguing. How do pills find their way to where they need to go? They must know exactly where to go and what they're there to cure when I swallow them.

I talk to pills before I swallow them. Why not? I say Right Paracetamols, find your way to the place in my head where it hurts. And I tap it to show them. I do the same with my knee, saying Make sure you go to my left knee that's got the pain, not the right one. And they do.

I've swallowed two Paracetemols.

What now? I'm waiting. I think hard about them dropping down my throat towards my stomach. One's stuck on a ledge half way down and I'm choking a bit, so I drink mango squash to wash it down.

By now the pills must be in my stomach getting swished and mixed up with the cheese sandwich I ate.

Pills don't last long because they get dissolved in what's called Bile. After that it must be even harder for them to know where they're going because they're just part of a mess of cheese sandwich and stomach chemicals and mango squash.

Dad's encyclopedia said I've got 100,000 miles of tubes and veins in my body and if I stretched them out they'd go three times round the world. So my pills must have to travel faster than a satellite round the planet to make my headache better in time or to stop the pain in my knee.

Maybe pills are cleverer than we think, they take short cuts.

Are there signs inside me telling pills where to go? This way for the lungs! Turn off here for the liver! Next junction for the kidneys! Straight through for the intestines! I imagine my pills gurgling through a tangle of motorway veins, ignoring the turn off for my bottom parts, then whizzing down tinier and tinier tubes like tiny country lanes with grass in the middle, all the way down to my left knee.

And how do pills know where there's a pain to cure?

Once when I put ointment on my flakey bottom mum said Make sure you wash your hands, son. But I didn't. Did the ointment try to cure flakey skin on my fingers where there wasn't any? Intriguing.

And what does pain look like? How do pills recognise it? Does pain call out I'm over here! Come and make me better!

Sometimes a Thinking Day leaves me exhausted. It has today.

Rumble noises up the road. Smoke. A motorbike and sidecar. It's black and old and rattles, and bumps up on the grass and I have to jump out of the way.

The rider takes off his goggles and says You with the limp again.

And you're Mr Hardaker who made me walk five miles back to Lars when your friend Mr Rawson wasn't in.

Let's go and see him now.

Will he be in? I ask.

How should I know? He says.

Why not. I jump in the sidecar and we're off.

I'm wearing the goggles again. Everything's orange and this time I'm a soldier in a Roman chariot waving a sword. I fall out at a corner but Mr Hardaker doesn't stop and I have to run to catch up and leap back into the sidecar.

After five miles we get to a church on a hill.

Are we going to a service? I ask him. I don't think I want to pray. Dad said praying's just hoping for things that never happen. Never rely on God, son, he told me.

Dad didn't think much of God. Or vicars. Reverend Des called at our house once while dad was watching the cup final, and stayed for tea. He ate all the biscuits, and went on and on about being holy, and dad missed the presentation of the cup.

I don't think dad really minded, though, he supported the other team.

I'm puzzled. Mr Rawson hasn't got a vicar's uniform on, he's wearing a string vest, an old brown sack and army boots. If he's a vicar where's his white collar? And his church isn't full of crosses, candles and smells like ours. And there aren't any guitars and tambourines and children's chairs and tables and nursery school Bible pictures on the walls, so it's not Happy Clappy either. In fact it doesn't look holy at all. I don't think there'll be a service because the prayer books and Bibles have all gone mouldy and they're propping up tables.

Mr Rawson's hitting a block of stone with a mallet as if he's very angry with it. Mr Hardaker points at a bunch of chisels poking out of a filthy cloth.

They look like cod gasping for air, he says.

I wobble my arms like fish fins and pout like a trout but no one laughs.

I think what Mr Hardaker said about the chisels is what's called an Analogy, which means Like. I'll have to learn about Analogies properly if I'm to be a poet.

Is this Mr Rawson's church? I ask. And is he the vicar? He doesn't dress like one.

Church is redundant, says Mr Hardaker.

Poor Mr Rawson. If he's out of a job it's no wonder his church is empty and looks a mess. And he's got no old ladies like Granny Gibbons wearing pearls and with veins in her hands arranging flowers and polishing the brass.

If Mr Rawson lives here and it's not a church any longer it doesn't look much of a house either. There are no sofas or cupboards with china and ornaments like mum and dad's. It's got old blankets for curtains and it's damp and musty. If mum were here she'd tell me to get a scrubbing brush out and give it a good going over with Vim. Reverend Des wouldn't. He thinks the Holy Spirit would blow all the dust away because God likes a tidy church.

I sit in a pew and have to scrape bird droppings off my trousers.

If Mr Rawson lives here he must sleep in the sleeping bag on the floor that looks like a pupa that a giant moth's crawled out of.

He's sweating so much hitting the stone that he's got a white face pack like Sally when I visited her once and she didn't know I was coming. When she opened the door I said You look like you've seen a ghost, Sally. And she went Whooo whooo and waved her arms and we laughed.

Bernhard's got wavy hair that flops like mum's custard, but my hair's bristly and crinkly and won't flop. Sally said Bernhard's quiffy hair is like waves at the seaside. A wave's coming in, Bernhard, she'd say, and run her fingers through his flops. I sang I do like to be beside the seaside and Sally joined in, but not Bernhard.

Sally never runs her fingers through my hair. Bernhard said if she did she'd cut her fingers and have to go to A&E.

What's Mr Rawson making? I ask.

Probably another platitude, says Mr Hardaker.

A duck-billed platitude? I say.

I've made another joke. It's a good one but Mr Hardaker doesn't laugh and nor does Mr Rawson. Mr Hardaker's ears are big but they don't do much listening. I talk loud to mum and dad at the Home, because they're deaf or because their batteries have run out. Once when I was there I said very loud How are you feeling? and the old man who farts in the next room shouted Mustn't grumble, I need the potty.

I'm intrigued by Mr Rawson. I whisper Do you think Mr Rawson is actually Mrs Rawson? He looks like a lady in his dress.

No idea, says Mr Hardaker. Anyway, it's an artist's smock.

I look hard at Mr Rawson's face which really is like a lady's with all the white make up dust. He looks like the Russian ladies in the Olympics. They have men's faces, and some of them look more like their husbands than their husbands.

Is Mr Rawson Russian? I ask. Where's he from?

Canterbury, Kilmarnock or Katowice. Who knows? says Mr Hardaker,

It's important to know if he's a he or a she, I tell him. If I call him Mr Rawson and she's Mrs Rawson it's not polite. Let's find out, says Mr Hardaker and pokes Mr or Mrs Rawson in the chest.

No breasts, he says. And no jimmy bulge in his trousers. I took him down the Tinners once and poured six pints of beer down him. Waited to see whether he went into the gents or ladies. He didn't go into either, so he or she must have a bladder the size of a football.

I notice that Mr Rawson wears goggles that make her

79

look like a man. They're not pink like a lady's. And he's got a beard. But so did Aunt Megs, and she propagated children so must have been a lady.

I whisper Does Mr or Mrs Rawson always use Jesus's holy altar as a work bench?

She, says Mr Hardaker, worships at the shrine of civic art. The ecclesiastical ambience is entirely appropriate to an artist of his standing.

What's his first name? I ask.

Lord knows. Bob? Gregoriev? Victor? Greta?

And what's she carving? I ask. It doesn't look like the statue of the dolphin in the park or the man on a galloping horse outside the town hall.

It's the base for a sculpture, says Mr Hardaker. Rawson's famed for his pedestals. Plinths par excellence. She'll spend a fortnight on it, carving the tiers, adding decoration, motifs contemporary and classical. Nothing's too good for his pedestals, the best marble, exacting workmanship. She works at the cutting edge, does our Rawson. By the time he's finished with it, that plinth will be fit for a Michelangelo or a Frink.

I've heard of Michael Angelo. But I don't know what a frink is. Already there are a lot of new words to look up in my dictionary - ambience, plinth, pedestal, frink. You never stop learning, even someone with all my wisdom.

I'm bored so I sit on a hassock. Dust puffs in the air all around. I'm choking.

Why does he or she spend all his time on the base and not the sculpture? I ask.

Immortality, old chap, says Mr Hardaker. Want to achieve immortality in art? Create a work that won't offend, that never sets itself up as an icon to be laid waste by whatever dictator or despot comes along in a millennium or so's time. New regimes destroy statues, not the pedestals they stand on. Rawson's plinths are destined for true immortality. Ah, the mistress speaks!

Tea, anyone? Mr or Mrs Rawson drops his chisel in the dust and holds up a kettle. She hands out jam jars of tea and a chipped plate with ginger biscuits from the cupboard by the holy altar. They're soft and dusty, but it's no crisis. I eat four.

I like this church even if it isn't very holy.

After tea Mr Hardaker had urgent business in the opposite direction and I walked five miles back to Lars.

I'm following a funeral. There are lots of black cars with people in them wearing black. It's very slow, and I'm hoping it's not going all the way to Budleigh Salterton. Helen could be dead herself before I return her book.

It's very rude to overtake a funeral. You have to respect the dead even though they are dead and don't know whether you're respecting them or not. Why do we respect dead people and not living people? People are nasty to people when they're alive then respect them when they're dead. Maybe if everyone was dead the world would be a politer place.

The people in the cars look very sad. When Aunt Megs died dad said he wanted to give her a good send off, but I don't think he knew where he was sending her off to. Even the Pope doesn't know, and he's God's representative on Earth. Nor does Reverend Des.

Everyone looked sad at Aunt Megs' funeral. Then at

the hotel after they'd sent her off wherever she was going they all laughed and talked about their operations and holidays. I don't go on holidays, my life's a holiday, so I ate lots of cakes, and prawns balanced on tiny biscuits that kept dropping on the carpet and getting covered in fluff. I kicked the prawns under a chair.

Uncle Bob asked me How are you doing, son?

I said Fine, thank you, Uncle Bob.

But am I? How should I know how I'm doing? I think I'm doing very well, but I'm not prime minister so Uncle Bob might not think I'm doing very well at all. A better question would have been What are you doing, son? Then I could have told him that I'm an entertainer and comedian, a poet, a Student of Language, and I'm thinking of becoming a psychiatrist and possibly a philosopher.

I asked Uncle Bob What are you doing, Uncle Bob? He looked puzzled.

Doing when? he asked.

In your life. Or what's left of it, because you're old now and you've probably got what are called Medical Conditions.

He frowned and raised his fists.

Well, young man, if you must know … a round or two of golf each week, line dancing on Thursday evenings, making balsa models … er …

Look, don't worry if you're feeling a bit of a failure, Uncle Bob, I tell him and give him a pat on the back. Not everyone can be prime minister before they die.

I meant this to be reassuring but Uncle Bob looked very cross indeed and went off to get another drink. I stood behind a plant and ate more cakes. You get good cakes at a funeral.

I'm overtaking the funeral. I'm behind a black car, and now I'm in front of it. Lars and I cycle slowly so the people wearing black inside the car won't notice us creeping by.

I creep past another car so slowly I fall off and everyone stops while I straighten Lars's handlebars and put his chain back on.

I creep past cars all the way up to the front until I get to the long black car called a Hearse with the dead person in. The men inside are wearing top hats. They don't look very sad at all, they're all laughing. Maybe it's just a job. Which it would have to be, otherwise they'd be miserable all the time and their wives would get fed up and leave them. Maybe they're laughing about funny things that happen at funerals. They must practice looking sad in front of a mirror.

One of them gives me a wink as I creep by. I wink back but he can't see it because the only eye I can wink with is on the other side of my face. Maybe the dead person in the coffin winked at me too, if the Christians are right and there is Life after Death.

I'm what they call Counting My Lucky Stars, which is what people do when they see a funeral car, because I'm not dead like the dead person in the coffin. I cycle on and wobble about on Lars, munching my Twix. I crash into a hedge and Ken the iguana's tail falls off because I forgot it was broken and held on with sellotape.

I'm pushing boundaries. I'm having something completely different for dinner. It's what they call an

Indian. Indian takeaways sell Indians. They're also called curries. A curry's very hot with rice and crackly leaves you crunch on. Bernhard's greedy. He stuffed so many Indian leaves in his mouth he choked and spat them over Sally's carpet then trod them in. I had fishcake and chips and a gherkin and didn't drop any. I don't waste food.

I'm outside The Taj Mahal, which I thought was a big palace in India and a bit like Vic and Brenda's wedding cake, which had as many what are called Tiers as an office block has stories. It lasted longer than Vic and Brenda's marriage, which was just a week. There's a picture of the Taj Mahal in my Book of World Wonders. It's beautiful. But this Taj Mahal's a tiny gloomy looking shop next to the post office with a flashing sign that doesn't flash properly and says Indian akeaways.

Are there chip shops in India called Buckingham Palace? And do their customers order an English? It's intriguing.

There's nothing in the window saying they're selling Indians or curries. This shop could be selling lawnmowers or shampoo. I hope not, I'm hungry.

I watch people going into the Indian and other people coming out carrying plastic bags. I'm hungrier every minute. Time to go inside.

This Taj Mahal's not like a proper shop with shelves stuffed with things to sell. It's more like the waiting room at the doctor's. There are chairs all round the sides with people sitting on them looking bored, all staring at their mobiles or at the telly on the wall, though the sound's turned right down.

A man comes out from a room at the back carrying plastic bags with Indians in. He shouts something and a lady gets up and takes the bags and leaves. The man goes in the back room then comes out again with more plastic bags, shouts something, and a man gets up, takes the bags and leaves.

What am I supposed to do to get my Indian? It's easy at the chip shop. You go in and say Chips and a gherkin please, and you pay and go outside and eat them.

When do I get my plastic bag with an Indian in?

Hours pass. People keep coming in and going straight up to the counter and getting served first. They're jumping the queue, which is not very polite. But no one sitting in the chairs seems to mind, which is curious. How does the man know what food they want? He must, because he hands them a plastic bag with an Indian in and they give him money and then go. And they don't come back complaining that it's not what they ordered.

My tummy's rumbling. The lady next to me says You have to go up to the counter to order your food, young man, there's a menu on the counter.

The menu's stuck down with sellotape. There are lots of words that must be Indian foods called Murgh Pakora, Puri Wrap, Sabzi Pokora, Mix Sabzi Platter, Bhaji Chat Masala, Dansak (mild), and Dopiaza (medium). Which ones come with chips? How should I know? The man holds up a notebook and pen and looks at me. I tell him I'm very hungry.

What numbers? he says.

Numbers?

Give me numbers, please, sir, he says.

How do I know what numbers? I want chips and an Indian. But chips aren't Indian and they aren't called Bhunas or Pokoras. I look at the menu again. It's confusing. The Indian man looks at me again and says Give me numbers, please, sir.

I look at the menu again. I tell him the numbers on the cows' bottoms – why not? – and he writes them down on his pad. I think he's puzzled. He adds up the prices and says £22, sir.

I'm shocked! Chips and a gherkin only cost £2.50. But I am pushing boundaries and exploring a new Culinary Experience so it's no crisis.

All for you, sir? the Indian man asks. You've ordered five main courses.

I tell him I'm very hungry and people sitting on the chairs start laughing. I'm happy, I'm being an entertainer and brightening their dull lives. I hand him money from my purse and he goes into the back room and I sit down again.

I watch the telly. It's got flickery pictures of people sitting in chairs on a stage looking angry. The audience look angry too. A fat lady comes on the stage in a t-shirt that doesn't cover her bosoms and everyone claps. She looks angry and shouts at a bald man in a string vest with tattoos sitting on a chair on the stage. The audience clap again then shout, and the man in the string vest gets angry and raises his fist and punches a man on another chair. Now all the people on the chairs on the stage are shouting and punching him. Then the lady in the t-shirt and the man with tattoos punch each other and then they cuddle and cry and everyone claps and women in the audience cry too.

Which is very curious indeed.

People on the telly are odd. Maybe I need to practice being odd if I want to go on telly.

The man behind the counter comes out from the back room carrying five plastic bags and shouts something. The nice lady nudges me and says That's you, young man, that's your Indian. I take the bags and the people sitting on the chairs clap and cheer and watch me leave.

I sit on the village green and open my bags. Inside are lots of plastic containers full of brown liquid with bits in, and piles of yellow rice a bit like the maggots dad took fishing. I eat what's in the plastic containers one at a time and by the third I'm feeling very ill. And there weren't any chips.

I sick it all up on the village green. It's a mess! I don't drop litter, it's not civilised, so I scoop it all back in the plastic containers and dump them in the rubbish bin. The Indian doesn't look any different from when I took the paper lids off in the first place.

I won't eat an Indian again, you know where you are with chips and a gherkin.

On Sunday afternoon's I'd lie on Sally's sofa listening to her Japanese music. I tried to like it because Sally does, but I wouldn't bother listening to it if I wasn't at Sally's. Sometimes it made me fall sleep.

Once when I woke the Japanese music had stopped but there were noises coming from Sally's bedroom. Moaning noises, and screamy sounds that got louder and louder then stopped suddenly. I was just about to rush in thinking Sally was ill when the door opened and Bernhard came out.

Is Sally okay? I heard screaming.

She certainly is, said Bernhard, and gave me a smirk.

I've been listening to Sally's Japanese music, I said to him. I fell asleep, then I woke and heard funny noises from Sally's bedroom.

Bernhard laughed and said it was Mongolian throat music.

I said it didn't sound as nice as Sally's Japanese music.

I wouldn't say that, said Bernhard, and made gobbling noises. In fact, it was Sally's music, she loves it. And he laughed in a nasty way and Sally came out and punched him.

If Sally likes Mongolian throat music so much maybe I should try to like it too. I told Bernhard I'd like to hear more of it, it was intriguing.

There'll be another performance tonight if I play my cards right, said Bernhard, and Sally punched him again.

I don't think Sally really liked Bernhard much at all. Except for his quiffy hair.

I like big bands and trombones and Elvis. But that's because it's what dad played on our radio. Dad told me Son, It's Now or Never, don't forget that. And I haven't. That's why I'm on my way to Helen's to return her book.

Lars has got a puncture. I need glue and a rubber patch, and quick, I've got to get to Helen's.

I need a lift to the shops. I Hail cars as they whizz by. At last one stops. It's small and Lars won't fit in, so I hide him in the ditch. I ask the driver if he's going to Budleigh Salterton, and he says Never heard of it, chum.

We whizz to the shops and I tell him about Lars's puncture and that I'm cycling to Helen's to return her book but he's not listening. He's telling me how sad his life is and that his wife's left him. I don't listen either. And I don't blame her for leaving.

We park in a big car park and he says Go to Halfords over there next to Argos. Be back here in half an hour, I'll be in Sainsburys.

Halfords is big and puncture outfits are small so it's like searching for a tiny creature in my microscope. Except tiny creatures wave their legs and say Here we are and puncture outfits don't.

I wish they could say where they are. I bet they're waiting for someone to buy them so they can mend a puncture, which is what they're meant to do. Being stuck on a shelf is no life, not even for a puncture outfit. It's curious to think of all the things on shelves in shops no one wants. They must all be shouting Buy me, here I am! Choose me!

But no one does. And they get old and forgotten and their boxes fade and they never get to do the things they were invented for. And new inventions are invented and they become what's called Obsolete and get thrown out. Very sad.

Where are the puncture outfits? I go past cycling gloves, spanners, engine oil, batteries, bulbs. At last! I choose the one at the back of the shelf that's been waiting the longest to get bought.

The lady at the till points the puncture outfit at her machine and it makes a pip pip noise. She says You've got a puncture, then.

Not me, I tell her, Lars has, and she laughs. She gives me a plastic bag to put it in, which I'll use for my dirty underpants.

Time to go back to the man's car for my lift back to

Lars. Where's his car? It's silver, and there are hundreds of silver and grey cars in the car park. They all look the same. Dad says in the Good Old Days all cars were black, so car parks must have looked just as confusing, but also gloomy like funerals.

When I die I hope Sally will come to my funeral. Who else? Some other people will come, but as most of them are older than me they'll probably die first. So it could just be Sally, but it's no crisis, I'll be dead so I won't know.

I don't think I'd like what dad called the Good Old Days. Dad says you had to put up with what you got and get on with it, so they can't have been that good if what you got wasn't.

There's the man! He's pushing his trolley. It's empty so he didn't spot any bargains. He finds his car straight away. He looks angry and kicks it and says his bloody wife has cancelled his card so he can't get any bloody money out and his petrol tank's nearly empty so he won't be able to drive me back to Lars. He swears and shouts and a man in uniform comes over and says Now sir, calm down, we can't go around swearing, can we?

I walk miles back to Lars. I'm too tired to fix his puncture, and I camp in the ditch. I've made cup-a-soup and dipped cheese triangles in it. They melted and didn't taste very nice. But you need to push boundaries, especially culinary ones. That's how men got to the moon.

I'm mending Lars's puncture. While I wait for the glue to dry I look at a twig. It's intriguing, it's got tiny insects crawling over its leaves. They all flew off and there was just the twig to look at, which wasn't as interesting.

I'm still watching the twig but nothing has happened so I'm stopping, it's Twix time.

Zen monks say if you look hard at Nature for long enough you forget yourself. I'm not sure I want to forget myself, I like me just the way I am.

But I was looking at the twig for a long time, so I'm trying to do some remembering just in case I have forgotten myself. I remember that I know Helen's address, and that Nils is a chair and sometimes a table, and that I like pound shops more than supermarkets, and that Aunt Megs is dead.

But how good is my memory? I need to think of something to remember that I may have forgotten. Which is difficult. To use an Analogy, it's Putting the Cart Before the Horse.

It's intriguing, there are things you can't forget. I don't have to remember I'm a man and not a woman because I pee through a willy. I also know I must once have been small boy because my real mum couldn't have propagated me the size I am now without bursting.

I've been thinking about Helen. I hope she's got a good memory, otherwise she may have completely forgotten about her hamster book. What happens if I get to 33 Riverside Close, Budleigh Salterton and I say Hello, Helen, I've come to return your book.

She says What book's that?

I say Your book about hamsters.

And she says Never seen it before and shuts the door.

I hope Sally's got a good memory and hasn't forgotten me.

This morning I cycled up behind another cyclist. I overtook him, and then had a rest and a bite on my Twix a bit further on.

He overtook me again.

I overtook him again.

He overtook me again.

I overtook him again.

This is silly, he said, let's ride together. I asked where he was going and he said I'm off to watch cricket.

He cycled on the inside all the time and I kept getting blown off Lars by lorries and he laughed.

Then he said Let's change over. I cycled on the inside and kept getting my wheels stuck in the drains and falling off and he laughed again. He was clever, because he made us change over on a quiet road where there weren't any lorries to knock him off.

Then I said Let's change over again, and we did, and he got his wheel stuck in a drain and it buckled and spokes fell out and he fell off, and I laughed and said Goodbye, can't stop, I'm in a hurry to get to Helen's to return her book. And he said You little Shit, very loud. Fuck off.

And I did, very fast. I cycled on and he didn't overtake me again. You meet all sorts.

I keep looking behind to see if he's catching up. There he is! I hide Lars in a bush and jump in the ditch and watch him cycle by. His wheel's buckled and he's wobbling all over the road. I hope the cricket isn't at Budleigh Salterton, he's not the sort I want to keep overtaking.

My mobile's beeped. There's a message from someone called EE. It says Hello GG1276. To update press here.

I did but nothing happened and I don't think it was Sally telling me how she is.

When I think about it I don't think it was Sally at all, unless she's changed her name. I think Sally's a nice name and suits her. I wouldn't change it if I was called Sally.

Who is GG1276? Maybe the message has gone to the wrong mobile.

It's June. Today's the longest day.

I cycled all day and it was very hot. In the afternoon I got dazzled by what poets like Wordworth call the Golden Orb of the Heavens. I thought it looked more like a lump of custard. I might use that in my next poem, but I don't think it's as poetic.

I'm camping. I don't like pitching my tent among all the big tents and caravans. They all stare at me and laugh. I feel like one of the tiny wriggly things I watch through my microscope.

I get into bed early, I'm tired. But it's still light and the longest day feels much too long already.

I can't sleep. There are noisy people in the next tent. They're laughing and shouting. I call out to them to quieten down but they don't hear me. So I put my trousers back on and go outside to their tent. You can't knock on canvas so I poke my head through a gap.

I'm shocked. There are two men and three ladies inside with no clothes on.

One of the girls screams and shouts Piss off you fucking pervert!

I say Excuse me, good people, would you mind being quiet as I'm trying to sleep.

One of the men says Chill, dude, we're celebrating the

longest day.

And the longest night if our luck's in, says the other man. They all laugh, so it must have been a joke.

I explain to them that all days are actually the same length, it's just that it's day for longer than night on the longest day. I would appreciate some cooperation as I'm trying to sleep because I've got to get to Helen's to return her book.

They start singing again and one of the men says Relax, dude, enjoy the light.

I tell them it may be light but it's really night. And it's bedtime and they should be sleeping too.

One of the men has got a huge willy, almost as long as my measuring stick.

He says Push off you little shit, and tries to punch me and falls over and belches and they all laugh.

Move your fucking tent, dude, he says and tries to punch me again.

I don't think they'll be getting a good night's sleep jammed together like that.

But it's hard to feel sorry for rude people.

I've moved my tent because of the noise, which now includes lots of moaning and screams like I heard at Sally's. Just like her Mongolian throat music, which is curious.

I'm putting it up in the trees.

I'm surrounded by giant plants with white flowers the shape of rockets. It's like a secret garden and I'm glad I moved here, it feels private and safe.

A man walking his dog in long shorts and a t-shirt saying Senior not Senile has a wee behind a tree.

He says I wouldn't camp here if I were you, sonny. Japanese Knot Weed grows fast. It grows through concrete. Its roots will creep under your tent in the night and when you wake up in the morning it'll be ten feet tall like a jungle, and you won't be able to fight your way out. Not trying to scare you, but you could end up a dead'n. When he goes off I see the back of his t-shirt says Retired not Expired.

It's after midnight now and proper night, but still quite light. I hope Knot Weed doesn't tangle and smother me like a fly in a spider's web. I've kept my trousers on in case I have to make a quick escape.

I wish I had a machete like jungle savages use in the Amazon, but all I've got is nail scissors from a Christmas cracker.

It's still day though it's really night. I can't sleep and I'm thinking hard about the longest day.

Today actually isn't the longest day everywhere in the world. In some places it's tomorrow already, in others yesterday or the day before, depending where you are. And it's day all day at the North Pole, and night all day at the South Pole.

I think it's the longest day today where Sally lives. If I was at Sally's I'd want it to be, I like being at Sally's for as long as I can. But I don't think my invitation extends to staying at night.

I still can't sleep. I've remembered I'm Trending, and imagining people from all over the country coming down to visit me at the hut. Scottish people will be racing down the motorway from Glasgow, and Chinese flying over from China, if the Interior Design magazine sells to foreigners. But I'm not there, and it's my hut that's Open Plan on Steroids, not me, so it's no crisis.

All this thinking is stopping me sleeping. It's night but still light and the naked men and women are still shouting and screaming but from a lot further away.

It's dark at last and I'm still awake and very hot. I wouldn't want it like summer every day. My Twixes would melt.

I like winter. Some people feel sad in winter. I don't, my life is exactly how I want it, whatever the weather.

Winter days seem longer than summer days even though they're not. It's probably because it's cold and raining and you can't go out, so they just seem very long. The shortest day's in December, and it's probably not worth getting up at all then if you haven't got what are called Inner Resources like I have.

I've been dozing. Dozing isn't proper sleep, it's what old people do. They doze all the time because they're in the Winter of their Lives, and their days must seem very short, even the longest ones. But they have to have nurses to wake them up in case they miss lunch.

Aunt Megs did a lot of dozing. At her funeral Reverend Des said she was enjoying Eternal Rest. How did he know? I think listening to Reverend Des would be a good way to get to sleep. He talks in Bible language all the time, and I don't think people are really listening unless they're in church. And then they doze off.

At Aunt Megs' funeral Reverend Des said How

beautiful this world is in which we live, and how the all-wise God has appointed the different seasons, so rendering the earth fruitful, and we must thank him for his blessings. And how fortunate it was that Aunt Megs enjoyed the fruits of God's bountiful creation like flowers and gardening.

Aunt Megs actually liked horse racing and watching wrestling on the telly. I think Reverend Des got the wrong old person, he thought she was the lady next door. He must have talked in Bible language all the time, even at home in bed, because Mrs Des left him. I would.

Morning at last. Phew, the Japanese Knot Weed didn't tangle and strangle me. It's quiet here in the trees, but I can't stay forever, I've got to get to Helen's.

This road bends a lot. Bends and corners make roads more interesting. If roads are straight there's only one place to go, straight ahead. Bends and corners take you to places you don't know are there until you've gone round the corner. What's down there? I say to Ken the iguana when we're coming to a bend. My dictionary says that's what's called a Rhetorical Question because Ken can't answer.

I wouldn't want to have been a Roman. They made very straight roads, so must have really wanted to get to the places they were going, even though they'd never been to them before. They marched, One two, One two, massacring people on the way. They got all the way to Scotland then built a wall. Why stop at Scotland? I don't think there was a sign saying This is Scotland, Keep Out! Maybe men in kilts playing bagpipes put them off. They would me.

The wall was made by someone called Adrian. He must have been a big builder to build a wall that long. And because they didn't have bends in their roads the Romans never knew all the great places round corners they were missing like Cornwall and Legoland.

I'd like my own wall round the hut like Adrian's. It would stop me Trending.

My walks round the combe all have bends. I tried to walk in a circle once but trees got in the way and barbed wire and angry bulls. If I drew a map of my walks they'd look like dried up prunes. I call my walks Prunes, and I've got 12. When Sally comes I say Let's go for a walk, Sally, pick a prune. And she does. Last time it was Prune 5. It's not my best walk, but it was this time because it was with Sally. I saw a woodpecker but Sally missed it as she was cleaning mud off her sandals.

I'm cycling fast round this bend. Woooooh, crash, I've banged into someone.

An old man. I hope he's not dead.

He smells of unpleasant things. A dead rabbit, rubbish bins, and Sally's dog Kevin's breath.

He opens his eyes and gets up, and crawlies fly out of his coat. He's not dead, which is lucky.

I am very sorry, sir, I say.

He's angry. His face is covered in white hair and he's got a beard like mum's old kitchen mop and a nose like a meringue. He's wearing a thick overcoat. I'm in my t-shirt and I'm sizzling.

You should look where you're going, he says.

I was, but I can't see round corners. Are you a tramp?

Certainly not, I'm a Gentleman of the Road.

What's that?

I go where it takes me.

That's just straight ahead. Don't you ever turn off at corners and go somewhere different and more interesting?

Never, he says. I like straight roads. Who wants to walk further than you have to get to where you're going?

Have you got a job? I ask. People like talking about their jobs and it might make him forget I've just knocked him over.

I mend nuclear power stations.

Intriguing. How? I ask him.

With my bare hands. And where are you off to in such a hurry, young man?

I'm cycling to Budleigh Salterton to return Helen's book.

You've made me tear my coat, he says. You'll have to pay for a new one.

But your coat was old and torn anyway. Show me the tear I caused, I tell him. I'm not paying for tears I didn't. Your coat looks like a coat from a jumble sale. We'd need to find another jumble sale, and they're held on Saturdays and it's only Tuesday.

I got it from Savile Row, he says.

I'm not surprised Mr Row threw it away.

I give him two pounds and tell him I'm in a hurry because I have to get to Budleigh Salterton. And I've twisted my ankle.

Look, he says, I can see you're a decent sort of chap. I'll return the book for you. We're not far from Budleigh. You wait here and rest your ankle, I'll borrow your bike.

This old man is a true Gentleman of the Road.

He jumps on Lars and cycles off in the wrong direction. Hey, I shout, you're going the wrong way! Helen's house is at 33 Riverside Close, Budleigh Salterton, but he doesn't turn round.

He's gone. He's stolen Lars. What's that in the ditch? Helen's book. It's muddy and a bit creased. And there's poor Ken the iguana with his face buried in the mud. I don't think that man was a Gentleman of the Road after all.

I'm walking now I haven't got Lars to ride on. Just up the road a lady keeps bending down then getting up.

She bends down again then gets up.

She bends down again then gets up.

I Hail her.

I'm never sure what to call ladies when you ask them a question. I wish she was a man because you can call men Chummy, Mate, Squire, Dude and lots of other names, they don't mind. Ladies are different because they do. The lady at the B&B at Minehead thought it was rude when I called her Old Lady.

I could call this lady Madam, Mrs, Miss or Ms. I'll have to call her something. If I just say What are you up to? that's rude too.

What are you up to, my good woman? I ask. I read this in a Penguin so I'm trying it out.

Do you smoke? she says. If you do I'll give you a good talking to. I'm picking up cigarette ends. I don't approve of litter. It's my small contribution to correcting the chaos in this troubled world.

You've missed that old newspaper, I say.

I specialise, she says, I don't collect newspapers. Do you approve of litter?

I don't, I tell her.

Then pick up paper, she says. You can start with that newspaper and anything else you see soiling our countryside.

So I do.

We're walking along together. She's putting cigarette ends in her bag. It's a big plastic one and she could walk all the way to Norfolk or Newcastle before she fills it. I wish I wasn't specialising in paper because my rucksack is already half full with newspapers and dirty tissues and sandwich packets with bits of old crust, and we've only walked two hundred yards. They're squashing my cheese triangles.

I've just found a magazine in the ditch with photos of naked ladies in. They're looking at me just like Sally looked at Bernhard when she was in the middle of doing his washing and he was in his underpants and she thought I was in the kitchen.

Wooooah, I say to the woman. I need to specialise too. Ring pulls, that's what I'll collect. I throw away all the bits of paper in the ditch and empty my rucksack.

I'm finding lots of old drinks cans. I rip off the ring pulls and hang them on a string round my neck. As I'm not specialising in cans I throw them back in the verge. After half an hour I've put together a silver necklace It's quite pretty, I'll save it for Sally. It feels good to be helping correct the chaos in this troubled world.

I'm looking at a View. It's what you do with Views. People mostly find Views at the top of hills, and when they spot one they stop their cars and look at it. I'd stop Lars if I was riding him but he's stolen.

I've been looking at the View for what feels like years. Views are too far away for you to do anything but look at them. They're like paintings except they're real and there's no frame round them. Sometimes when I'm looking at a View I make a frame with my fingers and screw up my eyes and it looks just like a painting. Is a View art? Does it have to be painted to be art? Who set what's art in stone anyway?

When I was looking at the View a lady walked by and said Lovely View.

I said Yes, it is.

And that was that. What else?

I don't think you talk about Views, you just look at them, so they're not very useful for practising Repartee. When the lady said Lovely View I don't think she wanted me to say anything, because she walked on and said it again to two old people in deckchairs eating egg sandwiches. The old lady nudged the old man to wake him up and he choked on his sandwich and said Lovely View and spat crumbs on his Daily Mail.

I've been thinking hard and I don't think saying Lovely View is a question at all. I could reply and say to the lady that the hills are intriguing or that the clouds look like mum has just wiped them with her dish cloth but I don't think she'd be listening. I wouldn't, either, I'd be too busy looking.

You can call Views Prospects. My dictionary says A Prospect is a Viewpoint Commanding an Extensive View of Landscape.

Not very enlightening. I've marked the page with my

fossilised kipper bookmark and I'll look at it again later.

Views are great places to visit to be on your own and contemplate the Wonders of Nature. No one else actually visits a View, they just look at it from a long way away. I've walked down the hill right into a View. Now I'm in it and part of it. I wave my arms to all the people looking at it from up on the hill. They're seeing me in the View but they don't wave back.

Now I'm here it doesn't feel like a View any longer, which is intriguing. But there's another View further on so I'll walk into that.

I've been walking into Views all afternoon. I've walked miles and eaten two Twixes and three cheese triangles. I think Views and Prospects are like rainbows. They're there but you never reach them because when you do they've moved further away.

I've been thinking hard. Who gave Helen's book to the jumble sale? Was it her mum? Mum emptied my cupboard of all my stuff when I left home to live in the hut and took it to a charity shop. I bought a few bits back then threw them away later when I realised I didn't want them.

I've been looking at Helen's book. I'd like to own it for both of us. I'm getting bored cycling to Budleigh Salterton, especially when I don't know where it is. It's like a View. I never seem to get there.

I've been buying Twixes in the village shop.

A lorry jerks to a stop just like a train. I hear a squeal but it doesn't sound like brakes. The driver's gone into the shop so I walk round the lorry looking for the squeal.

I've found it. The lorry ran over a rat so maybe the driver's gone for help.

The rat paws the air.
With milky eyes
It's swimming
In a sea of red blood

It's intriguing, poems start when you least expect them. It's called Inspiration and it's quite rare. Unless you're Wordworth who people say it happened too much to for the Good of English Literature.

The rat's staring up at me. What to do? Stamp on it? But I'm a vegetarian except when I'm eating corned beef on Ryvitas. I don't kill animals.

Here's the driver, he's eating a Twix bar like me and whistling. He sees me munching mine and winks and I wink back. I think he means Look at us both munching our Twixes.

Blood's bubbling out of the rat's fur, it's dying.

I call out to the driver You've run over a rat.

What's that, mate? He leans out of the lorry window.

You've run over a rat.

No charge, he says, grins, and winks again. I don't have time to wink back, he's driven off down the lane.

The rat's staring up at me.

Is it saying Kill me? Or save me? How should I know? There's a big stone mushroom by a gate along the lane. Even though I'm a vegetarian I drag it back, lift it up and drop it on the rat.

It's dead.

What the hell are you doing? A man runs over, he looks angry.

I just killed a rat. Put it out of its misery, even though I'm a vegetarian. It got run over by the lorry.

I'll give you kill a bloody rat! That staddle stone's our property. You've chipped it.

Howard, has he broken it? Has he broken our staddle? A lady with a plastic hat on runs up. She's got what looks like gravy all over her face but I think she's dyeing her hair. She's dyeing her face now too.

That's our staddle stone, she says.

I was killing a rat, I say. I used your mushroom to squash it.

A rat? Did he say a rat, Howard? Oh God, a rat! Where?

Under our staddle, Alice.

Under our staddle? Get rid of it, Howard. For God's sake get rid of it!

This lady's hysterical.

I roll the mushroom over. The rat looks a bit like a Full English Breakfast no one wanted. A tiny ugly dog's sniffing it and whining.

The man called Howard points at the dog and shouts Jess, inside. NOW.

He raises his fist and says That was no fucking rat, you idiot. That was Jess's pedigree pup. A teacup Chihuahua. It's worth five hundred pounds.

Not now, I tell him. It's not a teacup any longer, more like a saucer.

How was I to know? Poor Chihuahua.

I'm off to find a friendly View to walk in. It takes all sorts and sometimes I wish it didn't.

I'm standing under some pylons and writing another poem. These are the first lines.

Pylons, metal monsters,
Leafless trees
Marching across fields
Into the friendly View

It's my best so far. I might change the word Marching as I think it's what's called a cliché. Clichés are bad, there should be a spray to get rid of them. I'd press the button and say, Take that, cliché.

And pylons don't march, they stay still, you have to be sensible. But they can march in poetry, as poetry is an Exercise in Imagination. They make sizzling bacon noises which is probably Electric in the wires.

I wouldn't like to be a pylon. They're metal monsters stuck in one place and chained together like prisoners with long wires. I wouldn't want to be tied up with lots of other me's. There's just one me and I like it that way.

Birds don't like pylons. They travel thousands of miles from Africa then fly into them and die. Which is curious when they have all the sky to fly in then bump into wires which are very thin.

There should be signs on pylons saying Careful birds, watch out for the wires, stay away! But birds can't read signs. Better to show pictures of birds flying into electric wires and dying.

Do birds understand pictures?

I read somewhere that pylons give you headaches and cancer and wipe your memory, so it's best not to stand under them. I'm walking as fast as I can to get away from these ones and I'm Hyperventilating with the effort. Sally makes me Hyperventilate when she sits on the sofa with me and we play I Spy, and I say I spy with my little eye something beginning with S.

Sally looks all round the room and says Give up.

And I say, I spy you Sally. And we laugh.

I've passed them. I hope I haven't lost my memory because I don't want to forget Sally. I'm trying to remember if Sally has pylons near her house. I hope she doesn't walk under them and forget me. I'll text her some words through my mobile just in case.

I tap in some words. Hi Sally, don't walk under pylons. If you have, don't forget me.

That should do it.

Sometimes I wish I was a parcel. I'd address myself to Helen's and the postman would deliver me to 33 Riverside Close tomorrow morning. Postmen know where everywhere is. I'd just need brown paper and sellotape.

I'm Hailing to get a lift. A white van stops. On the side it says in big letters Actuating Logistics Solutions. The driver says Where to, chum? I tell him Budleigh Salterton and he says Jump in.

Now I can return Helen's book.

I'm puzzled. I ask him to explain what Logistics Solutions he's Actuating as it would be impolite to get my dictionary out. He says If my luck's anything to go by, bugger all. I've sixty parcels in the back to deliver before I go home.

I tell him I'll help. He gives me a Derek's Deliveries cap and says You can be my delivery man.

We drive hundreds of miles to places that aren't the ones we want to go to and Derek keeps swearing. He says people's houses are hard to find when you don't live there.

Derek's van has got a box on the dashboard called a Satnav. There's a picture of a map that moves when the van moves. I thought satnavs were soft curry things you get with an Indian. The box has got a lady's voice inside. She sounds nice.

I ask Where's she speaking from?

Derek says Out of her arse most of the time.

Which is a very impolite thing to say to a lady. I wouldn't talk to Derek at all if I were her.

She says Turn here, proceed for four hundred metres, turn left, then turn right in a hundred metres. Derek swears. They don't get on, but the lady doesn't lose her temper. I would.

Sometimes she knows where somewhere is, but not very often. But she sounds American, and America's thousands of miles away, so I'm not surprised.

I'm excited, I'm delivering my first parcel. The satnav lady says Drive down the lane, In a hundred metres turn left, You are approaching your destination.

How does she know? She's never been here before.

We drive across a river and through a farmyard. Derek runs over a chicken, then we stop in a field and get stuck. The lady says You have reached your destination.

I don't fucking think so, says Derek and swears at her.

She's calm and polite and says Turn round, Proceed up the lane, Take the second right in a hundred metres. Derek says Some people don't deserve having their fucking parcels delivered, and spits at the satnav box.

At last I'm delivering a parcel. I carry it through the front gate and knock on the door and say Parcel for you, lady. The lady says Thank you, young man, and shuts the door.

The next person's out.

Another lady says About bloody time.

Another lady in a see-through nightdress says Would you and your driver like a cup of tea? And maybe a little something extra?

I say Yes please, jammy dodgers, we'll eat them in the van. She slams the door. It takes all sorts.

The next person's out.

And the next.

And the next. Derek swears.

At the next I'm attacked by a dog. It rips the parcel and grins and I leave the bits on the doorstep. Derek says it's no crisis, it's a delivery.

It's dark when we get to Budleigh Salterton. I deliver three more parcels to people who aren't in. Derek says Don't they want their fucking parcels?

At last we're going to Helen's house. Where is Riverside Close? We drive around for hours and the satnav lady says do a U-turn, Proceed three hundred metres to the next junction. Derek swears and pulls out her plug. He drops me at 33 Riverside Close and says Good fucking luck, mate.

I ring the bell. If Helen's like most people she won't be in, she'll be somewhere else. A lady opens the door. I tell her I've come to return Helen's book.

Return it where? she says.

33 Riverside Close.

What book's that?

The book Helen says in red ink Please return to 33 Riverside Close, Budleigh Salterton. I hand her the book but it's not there, I've left it in Derek's van.

How can I help you, Derek? She points at my cap with Derek's Deliveries on.

I'm not Derek, I've just been helping him Actuate some Logistics Solutions. Are you Helen's mum?

Yes, I'm Mrs Jacobs.

I tell her when I get Helen's book back from Derek I'll give it back to her.

I'm afraid Helen doesn't live here any more, she says.

I'm yawning from not delivering so many parcels.

Come in and have some tea, you look tired.

We have cheese on toast and bakewell tart.

Where is Helen? I ask.

In a home.

Helen's mum looks sad.

Mum and dad are in a Home, I tell her, but they're old. Helen must be too young to be in a Home like them. She'll be wanting her children's book.

Helen's mum laughs. I don't think so, she's twenty. It's not that sort of home. Helen's not very well, and she's gone to a place where they can look after her.

When is she coming back?

She's not, I'm afraid.

I need to visit her to return her book.

Only family are allowed visits. But I can take it to her

if it's important. Where are you staying tonight? she says.

In my tent.

You won't find a camp site now, it's getting dark. You'd better stay the night.

I'm sleeping in what Helen's mum calls the Guest Room. There's a bed, a chair, and a dressing table, and that's all.

There's a picture of a seagull on the wall and I straighten it because it was flying upside down.

I take all the interesting stuff out of my rucksack and arrange it on the table and window sill. Ken the plastic iguana's balanced on the bed headboard. He keeps falling down, but it's no crisis.

I've woken up. It's early.

I creep out on the landing and the floorboards squeak. There are four doors. Which is Helen's room? The first is the bathroom. The one with the door closed must be Helen's mum's room. The next one's a cupboard. I open it up and it's filled with empty animal cages. Curious.

The last room must be Helen's. I want to see if she's got Penguins and a chair like Nils and lots of special stuff like me.

It's empty. Just another guest room with no guest. Helen's mum comes out yawning.

Is this Helen's room?

It was.

Where's all her interesting stuff? Like I've got Ken and my fossilised kipper.

Gone to her new home.

I show her how I straightened the photo of the seagull

111

because it was flying upside down.

Helen did that, she likes jokes. When did you last have a bath?

February, I tell her.

I thought so. I'll get you a towel.

Helen's mum's clever, how did she know I only have showers?

I'm in the bath. On a shelf are bottles called Miracle Hair Insurance, Restore and Control, and a tube called Body Butter. I use all of them except the Body Butter, which is a bit greasy. I feel better already now my hair's Insured, and I'm Restored and Controlled.

In the bath when I lift my legs out of the water the level goes up and when I put them back under the level goes down. Which is curious. I get out and remember I've forgotten to wash my down below parts, but it's no crisis. I'm hungry, you die of hunger not dirt.

Breakfast time but no sugar snapcrackles. I eat cornflakes and a twisty crumbly thing like a fossil, most of which goes on the floor.

Helen's mum says Tell me about the book.

I tell her it's a book on hamsters I found at a jumble sale near Minehead.

Ah, we had a holiday there when Helen was small and I remember she left it in the hotel. It upset her.

She'll be very happy to see it again, then.

No, no, best she doesn't see it. Helen's mum looks worried, very worried.

But Helen says she wants it back it in red ink.

Please, you mustn't give it back to her.

I explain I can't return it anyway, and nor can she because Derek's got it in his van, and Derek could be anywhere and probably is because of his satnav lady.

Helen's mum looks relieved.

I tell her it was impolite of me to look, but the cupboard upstairs is full of empty animal cages.

She looks worried again.

I can't bear to throw them out.

Cupboards are full of memories, I tell her.

Helen loved her hamsters, she says. She used to lie in her bed watching them for hours running round and round on their wheels. It made her happy. And calmer. But they all died from a virus very suddenly, and she was so sad it made her even more ill, and when the last one died she got ill and had to go into the home.

I tell her that my iguana died and I was very sad, so I know how Helen felt. And how Sally bought me a plastic iguana called Ken and I'm not so sad now.

After breakfast Helen's mum says Let's look at my plants, you worked in a garden centre.

The garden's mostly grass and weeds. She says Helen did all the gardening. She asks whether this plant or that plant likes light and I say Yes. She asks if this yellow flower likes shade and I say probably. They're not dead so they can't be that unhappy.

We stop for Twix time which is ginger biscuits. I stuff some in my rucksack for later.

I really need to visit Helen, I say.

It's family visits only, as I said. But here's the address if you want to write to her. But, please, don't give her the hamster book.

Time to go. I wave goodbye.

I'm off to visit Helen. I'll say I'm family, she needs her book. But I need to get it back from Derek first.

I'm walking along main roads now I can't cycle along them. To make life interesting I'm counting lamp posts. Lamp posts must be smelly, because Sally's dog Kevin likes smells and he smells every one we pass and lifts his leg and wees when Sally and I go shopping. I like Kevin so I've just tried sniffing a lamp post. One's enough, thank you. Kevin likes dog wee and I like Kevin, but we must like different smells. Are dogs' noses like tweezers? Can Kevin pick dog wee apart and say Ah, that bit's Rover, that bit's Henry?

If I was a dog I'd like to be Kevin. I'd snuggle up on Sally's lap and give her a lick like he does.

Dogs sniff other dogs' bottoms as well as peeing everywhere. Our Planet's just one big toilet for dogs. Aunt Meg's dog Winston smelt my bottom one Sunday then stole my pork chop. Aunt Megs said Isn't he a giggle, and laughed again when Winston did a number two on my rucksack.

When Aunt Megs died Winston was what they call Put Down. Which must have been a surprise because dad told him he was going to the vet for a shampoo.

Lamp posts all light up at the same time. One minute the road's dark and you can't see where you're going and the next it's lit up like an airplane runway. They must have alarm clocks inside that say Time to light up. And they all do.

Bernhard said we're being watched by lamp posts. All

the time wherever we go. Why? He says lamp posts have tiny cameras on them, and they're taking pictures of us that they send in electrical packets miles and miles away to people sitting in offices who are staring at hundreds of screens searching for criminals and terrorists. They've something called Software that compares your face to millions of others in less than a second. Then they press alarm buttons and police cars race towards you to arrest you and lock you up. Then they let you go because you're actually someone else.

I'm careful, I always point my face down when I pass lamp posts just in case.

I'm measuring the distance between lamp posts. They're the same number of steps apart then suddenly they're a different number. Dad says it's so drivers know what speed they can drive at. If they drive too fast they Collect Points and have to sell their cars and walk or catch buses or even go to prison.

When I think hard about it I don't think lamp posts are very friendly, even if they do Light Our Darkness. Maybe the people looking at screens in offices miles away are watching me measuring the distance between lamp posts. I hope they don't think I'm a terrorist. I haven't seen any police cars racing towards me.

Why have lamp posts in the country? Why light up a hedge? The foxes, birds, bats and badgers know exactly where they are.

Light's intriguing. God said Let there be light, and there was. He didn't just switch light on, He invented it. We know this because before He invented light the Bible says there was Eternal Darkness. How did God know what light was to invent?

I asked the Reverend Des but he didn't know, and he's read the whole of the Bible twice, even all the begatting bits where everyone's propagating all the time. Most things need light. Humans do, otherwise we'd all bump into each other in the dark because we haven't got what's called Night Vision like bats and badgers. It's lucky someone invented torches, though mine doesn't work because the batteries have gone mouldy.

It's important to entertain drivers who are late getting back home from their jobs and feeling angry and miserable with their sad lives. At the 203rd lamp post I stand underneath and have a shower in the yellow light pouring down on me. I give myself a good scrubbing down, including under arms and feet. A car hoots, jams on its brakes, and a van drives into the back of a mini.

Books need light. They're no use at all in the dark. If God hadn't invented light books wouldn't have been invented either. Sally reads books on what she calls her Tablet. You touch the glass and a page appears and you touch it again and the page turns over and all the words light up, which is very clever. Bernhard said a Tablet has got as many books inside it as a public library. He also said there's a postage stamp with the New Testament written on it. I don't think so, and I didn't at the time, and I told him.

I walk miles along the coast and imagine I'm on a seaside holiday with mum and dad. But it's too warm and sunny here. I always took my sun hat, bucket and spade and swimming trunks on family holidays, but spent most of the week sheltering under mum's umbrella wearing my raincoat. Once when I was waiting for mum I got trapped playing prisons in the turnstiles of the ladies' toilets, and they had to call the fire brigade to unjam them. No ladies could get in or out and I wasn't very popular. One gave me an ice cream because I was crying, but it made me cry more when she poked it through the bars and dropped it. I was on page three of the local paper.

It was always exciting arriving at the holiday camp, and seeing all the families outside their big caravans looking happy and cooking baked beans and playing shuttlecock. But our caravan was always the very last one, right at the far end of the site by the sewage works. It was small and old-fashioned and smelt of gas. I won a prize for whistling.

It's sandy, so I run along the beach and jump over the wooden fences called Groynes to keep fit. I've just landed on a lady sunbathing, and her bikini top fell off and blew away and she screamed. I picked it up out of a rock pool with a stick, and it had a crab hanging on it and she screamed again.

It's dark. I can't find a campsite so I'm sleeping in a bus shelter.

A bus stopped for ten minutes. It was empty and the driver kept looking at me waiting for me to get on, but I didn't and he gave me a rude sign and drove off.

I'm learning the bus times on the time table. You never know what knowledge you'll need and when you'll need it, dad said.

A sign on one side of the bus shelter says See this advert? Your customers will. Advertise now!

I'm thinking hard about advertising in the bus shelter

while I try to get to sleep.

I've woken up. It's morning. People are queuing for the bus and a lady's sitting on my feet. Dad said answers to questions come to you when you're asleep and he was right. I haven't got any customers so I won't advertise.

I buy more Twixes in a shop. A sign in the High Street says Meditation Classes, Everyone welcome, British Legion Hall, 10.30 Tuesdays.

It's Tuesday and 10.30 so why not?

Ladies in zebra stripe leotards are chatting about their holidays and operations. A lady whose leotard says Sweat is Magic says Welcome to our class! What are you hoping to achieve?

Universal Peace, I tell her.

A tough ask in fifty minutes, she says, but we'll give it a go.

I'm in the front row.

She says Right, we'll start with stretching exercises. Arms outstretched, bend forward, hold it, hold it, now bend back. Breathe in deeply, breathe out.

Arms outstretched, bend forward, hold it, hold it, now bend back Arms outstretched, bend forward, hold it, hold it, now bend back. Breathe in deeply, breathe out. Rest.

Now, touch your toes. Hold it ... Relax.

Right, sit cross legged. Close your eyes and let your thoughts come, then let them go.

I'm thinking bus times. Not very calming, especially the irregular Sunday and Bank Holiday services.

The lady's voice says Think of a special place you like

to be and imagine you're there.

I think BIKE, though it's not really a place.

I think hard about Lars's handlebars,

his wheel nuts,

his chain,

his saddle my bottom was sitting on till he was stolen,

his spokes, one of which is probably still broke.

The voice says Keep thinking of your special place. I'm running out of bits of Lars to think about, so I think of Sally. She's a special place even though she's a person. I'm on her sofa listening to her Japanese music but that's not very calming either, so I just think of Sally.

I've woken up.

Everyone's gone. Did I achieve Universal Peace? Who knows, I was asleep. Time to find Derek.

Mr Hardaker said if you stay in one place and wait long enough everything comes by in the end. A glacier will creep past from the Arctic and Cliff Richard will cycle by backwards wearing a fez. But by then I'd probably be dead or in a Home like mum and dad. I'm too busy to wait.

What now? I'll find a field, the satnav lady always takes Derek into fields.

I'm not in a field, I'm in a teashop. I'm hungry.

A waitress says Yes, young man?

I tell her I want tea and a cake because I'm hungry and I need to find Derek. She looks at her watch.

He'll be here in half an hour, she says.

That's lucky! I've found Derek already and didn't have

to wait till In the End like Mr Hardaker said I would.

Men who aren't Derek come in and drink coffee and read newspapers then leave.

The table cloth droops down to the floor. I'll be a magician and entertain the other customers while I wait. I'm about to whip the table cloth away and shout Abracadabra and amaze everyone when the waitress in the pinafore screams No! and everyone looks round and two old ladies in the corner give me looks. I give them looks back.

The teashop lady is Looking Me Up and Down. I tell her I slept in a bus shelter and I'm hungry and she says We're closing soon, you'll have to order quick.

Which is curious, it's only half past ten.

She brings me the cake stand but they don't look proper cakes. They're like tiny birds' nests you see in the hedge with tinier berries like eggs.

She says Take your order?

I'll have the blackbird nest, I say. She looks puzzled.

I point at the cake with blue berries on top.

One bite and it's gone. I call the waitress over and say I'd prefer a jumbo jam doughnut and she looks cross.

What about a sandwich? she says.

The sandwiches are tiny too, and they've no crusts. Crusts are vital for healthy teeth, and it's not just me saying it, it's dentists, so I tell her I'd prefer sandwiches with crusts on. She looks even crosser.

I'm a very patient person and like to help people, so I explain to her Without crusts your customers will get bad teeth and they won't come back, and your teashop will have to shut and you'll be on benefits like me.

She snarls like Kevin snarls when he gnaws Sally's slippers. She says Choose something quick and stop wasting my time.

I choose a meringue with frilly paper round it.

One bite and it's gone.

Can I have a cup of tea now? I say.

Assam or darjeeling? she asks.

Excuse me, I say in a friendly way, I did actually ask for tea.

Some people just don't listen.

There are flower and cottage pictures all over the walls and jugs and plates and china dolls arranged on shelves. I tell the teashop lady she must like jumble sales as much as me.

She looks cross again and brings a teapot like an old cottage with a thatched cosy. The cups are tinier than her cakes.

Can I have a mug? I ask her. I'm thirsty.

She says No you can't, this is an Old English tea shop and we have cups.

I tell her I don't think it's very Old English at all. For a start it's next door to a betting shop and launderette and it's not thatched and doesn't have roses round the door.

I slurp my tea as it's hot and the old ladies give me more looks. Old ladies don't like anything, they just moan about the world because it's Passed Them By.

Derek hasn't come in. The tea shop lady says he's probably not coming now and I should leave immediately.

I order a cream tea, just in case.

After half an hour the tea shop lady comes over and

says I thought you wanted to see Derek. He's there, sitting in the window. Just say what you've got to say then get out.

I look over. No he's not, I say.

She calls to a man in the window. Derek, this chap's been waiting for you.

He comes over. What can I do you for?

You're not Derek, I tell him. Derek's got a delivery van.

Ah, you mean Derek of Actuating Logistics Solutions. I saw his van. He's just delivered to the electrics shop down the road.

I'm feeling a bit sick from all the jam and cream and I rush to the toilet but there's only one and the two old ladies are queuing outside the door.

They'll take ages to go because the valves in their bladders are old and leaking. I'm jumping up and down. At last I rush in. The cream teas don't look very appetising when I sick them up down the toilet.

The tea shop lady gives me my bill. Nineteen pounds!

What do you expect for three cream teas and two fancies? she says. Piss off and don't come back.

Not very Old English.

The electric shop's got hoovers, TVs, radios and washing machines in the window.

A man wearing a brown coat says Can I help you, sir?

I tell him as I haven't got an electric socket in my tent, probably not. Have you seen Derek?

Derek who?

Derek's deliveries.

Been and gone, sir. I've got his mobile number.

I sit on a seat in the park and switch on my mobile. It makes noises and lights come on. I press the tiny phone picture and type in Derek's number which is quite like the numbers on the cow's bottoms.

Derek's Deliveries, Actuating Logistics Solutions countrywide.

Is that Derek?

None other.

You've got Helen's book.

Helen's what?

Her book.

Derek's mobile makes crackling noises. His word packets must be stuck in a mast somewhere and not travelling down into my mobile.

He says Missed that, say again. Shit, signal's breaking up, going under a bridge …

It's about Helen's book, I yell.

I'm back. Checking my roster. Can't see a delivery for anyone called Helen. Where am I supposed to be taking it? What's her surname and address?

Jacobs, Budleigh Salterton.

Can't see it on my list.

That's because Helen doesn't live there any more.

Story of my life, mate. Who the fuck is ever where they should be? So where do I deliver the damn book if I find it?

You're not delivering it.

Are you sodding me about?

It's me, remember? I left Helen's book in your van.

Signal's going … I'm stuck in a field. Bloody satnav, I'll kill that woman …

Where are you, Derek? Come back, I shout into my

phone. I need to pick Helen's book up, and quick.

Fuck knows where I am, mate. Satnav's on the blink. Signal's going ...

Derek's gone.

It's time to hitch a lift and find Derek again. The road's busy.

An old lady's hitching, and she's in front of me, waving her stick at cars. She looks a bit like a witch. The cars aren't stopping. I wouldn't, you don't give lifts to witches. But it's usually important to help old people, even witches, but because I'm in a hurry I move in front of her so cars see me first.

You're rude, young man, she shouts, and hits me with her stick.

Where are you hitching to? I ask.

Ain't hitching. Trying to cross the road. I need to get oven gloves from the shop. Lord, this traffic, I don't know if I'm coming or going. She twirls a long twisty hair on her chin.

I tell her if she hasn't been to the shop and bought the oven gloves she must be going not coming. Old people get confused. Dad does. Last time I visited he called me Jimmy Greaves and told me off for missing a penalty against Arsenal.

I'm baking a pie, she tells me. For dad.

A pie for her dad? Intriguing.

A pie for your dad. He must be very old, because you're almost as old as the hills. And they're very old.

Dad's two years younger than me, she says and hits me with her stick again.

I'm Quick on the Uptake but I'm confused.

Your dad propagated you before he was born?

No, dad's Bob, my husband. We been married these sixty year.

This old lady married her dad. She's madder than a witch. I need a lift out of here, and quick.

You shouldn't be hitching, I tell her. Or baking. You should be eating Meals on Wheels and watching daytime telly.

She hits me with her stick again.

I'm even more confused. I don't know if I'm coming or going now, but I definitely want to be going. This old woman needs help, from a Care Professional. Anyone whose dad's two years younger than her needs help.

Look, young man, just help me cross the road.

Cars are racing by both sides of the double white line.

White lines are clever, they're like very low fences that stop cars from crashing into each other when they pass. Farmers couldn't use them in fields because cows would just walk across them. That's because of the superior intelligence of humans over animals. Reverend Des calls it Man's Dominion Over Nature.

More cars whizz by. Are they coming or going? Most will be going as the drivers are on their way to work. Except those on night shift.

A tiny blue car skids to a stop just up the road. The driver's waving.

Want a ride? he shouts. Jump in.

I barge past the old lady and jump in.

I say I need to find Derek again so I can ...

Belt up, he says.

He's just out of short trousers. But it's important to

be polite to drivers giving you a lift, even if they do look under age, so I belt up and don't say anything.

Right, here we go! he shouts.

We're off. Going faster and faster. Everything's blurred, and lamp posts flash by faster than I can count. If we were a plane we'd be in Spain by Twix time. This car's noisy, I can't hear a thing, it's got no roof and I'm hanging on to my hair in case it blows off.

Just nicked it, he shouts, and taps the steering wheel. 911, convertible, water-cooled, variable valve timing, integrated sump. Feel that cornering? That's the independent MacPherson and Porsche traverse suspension struts.

We're skidding round bends faster than a spaceship round the planet, but I don't say anything because I've belted up.

It's a monster, he shouts. Feel that active all-wheel drive. Fucking awesome. And it's got custom four-piston aluminium caliper brakes and vented cross-drilled discs.

I don't think it's much of a car at all, it's only got two seats. If they'd left out the independent Macpherson struts there'd be room in the back for two more. This driver's definitely not a Family Man, even if he is too young to propagate one.

I can't belt up any longer. Are you old enough to drive? I ask him. You should be wearing short trousers. And where are we going? I need to find Derek so I can get Helen's book back.

He doesn't hear me because we've just broken the Sound Barrier. We've left my words far behind and I'm already looking around to see men in kilts.

I see a sign saying Budleigh Salterton two miles.

But Helen's doesn't live in Budleigh Salterton any more, I shout. I've just come from there.

A blue light's flashing behind us and we slow down using the four-piston monobloc aluminium caliper brakes.

Shit, he mutters. The Old Bill. Leave the talking to me. He opens the glove compartment and says Here, take this.

I look down, I'm holding a gun. But I don't say anything, I'm belted up and in shock.

A policeman leans in the window. Proceeding a little swiftly, weren't we, sir?

No choice, says the driver and points at me. He held me up.

Held you up, sir?

At gun point. Made me nick the car.

Car theft and illegal possession of a firearm, eh? Step out, young man. Hold 'em out.

I hold 'em out. I'm in handcuffs, not oven gloves.

I'm being driven to the police station. I tell the policemen that the last time I was in a police car it was Today to me, but their tomorrow. And my Today was their Yesterday. And their Tomorrow my Today. I explain this very carefully as they don't seem very Quick on the Uptake.

They lock the doors and drive faster.

I'm in the police station. At the desk the sergeant's taking all the special things out of my rucksack.

So, what have we here. Item: Twix bars (two), four cheese triangles (one squashed), an iguana (plastic, tail broken), a compass (from a cracker), pyjamas (striped, used tissues in pocket), mirror (pink, cracked), toy fire engine (fireman headless), tent with pegs, sleeping bag (stained), plastic knife, fork (prong missing), spoon. And what might this be, sir? A Scholl inner sole?

My fossilised kipper.

Bit of a comedian, are we, sir? Right, come with me.

I tell him I'm happy to proceed with him in an orderly fashion to the aforesaid destination. Wherever that is.

It's best to talk their language.

The policeman's taken my belt so my trousers keep falling down, but luckily there are no ladies to see.

We're in the Interview Room. A detective reaches across me and turns on a tape machine using the Long Arm of the Law as it's on the far side of the table.

Interview 13.26. DC Sturt and DC Reeves in attendance.

Name, sir?

No comment, I say.

I think that's what criminals say on the telly whether they're guilty or not.

Place of residence?

No comment.

Where did you acquire the firearm?

No comment.

Chatty, aren't we, sir? Anything at all to say for the tape?

I'm thinking hard. Maybe saying No Comment is rude. Dad told me Always tell the truth, son. I tell the detective I'm trying to find Derek to get Helen's book back, and Helen doesn't live in Budleigh Salterton any more, she's in a home, and she said in her book on hamsters Please return this book to Helen Jacobs, 23 Riverside Close, Budleigh Salterton, but Derek's got her book in his van and he's Actuating Logistics Solutions somewhere.

That's more like it, sir. Being cooperative could reduce your sentence. You're entitled to a brief, we can appoint one for you.

A brief what?

A legal adviser, sir. A solicitor.

I've always thought I think hard, but I'm thinking even harder now. Policemen are clever at finding missing persons. Maybe they can help me find Derek.

You could help me find Derek, I tell him. He's missing.

Missing for how long?

Derek's always missing.

And where do you think his whereabouts might be?

Probably in a field swearing at the satnav lady. She tells him where to go and he does, and then he gets angry and tells her where to go.

They've locked me in a cell. It's more comfy than my hut and warmer than the bus shelter. I'm waiting to be what they call Processed and Charged. A policeman's standing by the door guarding in case I try to escape.

Can I blow your whistle? I ask him.

We don't have whistles any more, we use mobiles.

What have you got inside all those pockets and pouches? I keep my favourite things in mine. What are your favourite things? And where's your helmet?

We don't have helmets, we wear caps.

Can I see your truncheon? It's a bit like the man's willy

129

at the campsite.

I'd be careful what you say, matey. It's not a truncheon, it's a baton. It extends. See? It snaps out when I shake it.

Can I measure the cell with it?

Okay, if it shuts you up. Trust my luck to get landed with a fucking lunatic at the end of my shift.

I measure the distance to the wash basin, then to the bed, then to the far wall. It measures ten and two bits truncheons. If I used my measuring stick it would be different, but the same length in External Reality. I explain to the policeman that this is why measuring's so intriguing. Everything measures differently depending on what you measure it with. This cell could be one piece of rope long or a hundred Magnum sticks.

He's yawning.

Am I boring you, constable?

You'd be bored too if you'd just finished a double shift two nights on the trot and you get stuck with a little snot like you.

I need the toilet. I tell the constable I'm feeling an Urge to do a number two, and quick.

For Christsakes. Come on then.

Can I measure the distance to the toilet? You can't know too much about what things measure.

Anything to shut you up.

I measure from the door of the cell along the corridor to the next cell using the extended baton. Then to the next. Then to the next, and then to the toilet. I sit down for a number two and try to not make gurgling noises.

When I come out he's leaning against the wall snoring.

I carry on measuring, from the toilet to the next cell, then to the next, then to the next, and then to my cell.

I've a sudden Urge to measure from my cell to the front desk. Urges are impossible to resist. The constable's snoring so he won't mind.

I measure from the cell to a cupboard where they probably keep the handcuffs. Then to the notice board covered in pictures of Wanted Men. Then to the front desk.

It's empty. I've another irresistible Urge, and I measure from the desk to the entrance door, and from the entrance door to the outside steps. It's taking much too long to get Processed and Charged, and I need to get to Helen's, and quick.

I'm outside. I've escaped. I don't hear any shouts, so it's no crisis.

I'm on the run. A Wanted Man.

I've been thinking about Time and how I wouldn't like serving it in prison.

The Reverend Des told us God created the world in seven days. How does he know? He says it's in the Bible, but the Bible was written years afterwards and whoever wrote it wasn't there at the time. Did God have a clock? He must have invented time first so he could measure it and know it took Him seven days to create. And why did it matter, God had no deadline, so it was no crisis.

Everyone's clocks and watches tell different times. Who knows which is right? Our church clock had the loudest ding, but it was always wrong so the congregation at Reverend Des's church ignored it. Which was a good job because they could turn up late for his sermons. Reverend Des droned on and on for hours till everyone was yawning and thinking about their Sunday roast. Half way through church was always Twix time, and Twix time waits for no man, not even a Man of God. I'd kneel down in the pew, hold a Twix between my two palms and nibble it, as if I was praying.

Dad said the Reverend Des liked the sound of his own voice because He believed it was the voice of God. No one knows what God sounds like, but I don't think He'd choose Reverend Des to be His voice.

Did God have a voice at all? When I think about it you only need a voice when there's someone else to say something to, and God lived on his own till he invented Adam and Eve. I don't think Adam and Eve knew what time it was as they're never wearing watches, they're naked in paintings, with just fig leaves over their bottom parts. And Eve never wears a brassiere in paintings like mum and Sally, so maybe she was the sort Aunt Megs called a Hussy, and that's why God threw her and Adam out of Paradise.

But maybe God droned on and on like Reverend Des, and Adam and Eve got fed up listening to Him and left Paradise.

Uncle Don had a watch called a Fob. He kept it in his blazer pocket and kept taking it out and looking at it and sighing. I think he was willing on the time for Aunt Megs to die. She did, too, quite soon. And so did Uncle Don.

Mum told dad once to Make Time to cut the lawn. Dad swore and said the damn grass grows faster than I can mow it and went out to his shed in a mood. Mum had to poke his pork chop under the door. I wanted to be helpful and went to the garden shop and asked the man if he had anything to stop grass growing. He sold me something called Roundup, and that stopped it growing for good. But mum and dad still weren't happy. You can't please everyone all the time, not even your parents.

I miss Sally. I don't miss Bernhard. He said I was a mummy's boy. I told him we're all mummy's boys, Bernhard. How else did we get propagated?

He laughed and asked me if I'd seen mum's dumplings. I said actually, Bernhard, I have, I ate them every week for Sunday dinner. He laughed again and said he meant mum's bosoms and bet I sucked milk out of them till I was in long trousers, and Sally hit him. I told him actually, Bernhard, I didn't think so, as I've got a very good memory.

Mum kept her bosoms inside a brassiere. They were private and I don't think she let even dad see them. I used mum's old brassiere as a catapult to shoot stones at the neighbour's cat. It twanged and the cat flew across the lawn and landed in the pond.

I'm thinking hard. Where can I stay now I'm on the run? There'll be police dogs after me and they won't be faithful friends licking my face and wanting me to throw sticks.

So I'm hiding in the woods. The police won't find me because it's summer. If it was winter there'd be no leaves on the trees and they'd spot me from a helicopter and shout through a microphone Come out with your hands above your head.

I wouldn't want to be a policeman. But I'd like to wear a policeman's uniform and have handcuffs and a baton and other important stuff like the spray that makes your eyes smart and go red. But not a detective, as they just wear jeans and t-shirts like everyone else and drive round in Unmarked Cars watching for people who they think look guilty, then arrest them and put handcuffs on them and say I think you'd better accompany us to the police station. Where's the fun in that? I like dressing up.

It's lucky I'm short. It makes me harder for the police to find.

My hair's grown long, though. I'm thinking of tying it in a bun like Sally does before she has a shower. Once when I went to see her she had just a towel on. I saw her legs. They were lovely, both of them. They disappeared up to a place under the towel I'd like to see very much but know it's not polite to ask. Sally doesn't have hair on her legs like men. Ladies don't grow much hair at all, except Aunt Megs, who had a bigger moustache than dad and looked like the grizzly I saw at the zoo.

I'd still like Sally if she had hairy legs.

Electricity makes hair stand on end. Mine does even without Electricity. I've always had a bristle brush on top. One day at Sally's Bernhard turned me upside down and dangled me by my legs and mopped up some soup he'd spilled on the floor, and Sally got angry and hit him. It was minestrone. I picked the bits out with her eyebrow tweezers and it took a long time because Sally buys very expensive soup from Waitrose which says it's a Nourishing Meal in a Tin. Which it would have been if Bernhard hadn't dropped it.

Bernhard said he knew a Turkish barber who could cut my hair. He and Sally took me into the high street for a haircut. The shop was what's called a Takeaway but Bernhard said the man did haircutting on the side. I made a joke. I said I hope he'll cut my hair on both sides, not just the one. Sally and I laughed. Bernhard didn't.

Ismail the Turkish Takeaway barber was even hairier than Bernhard. Bernhard said we could watch his beard grow while we waited. Ismail had to shave before breakfast, after lunch, and before Coronation Street, every day.

Ismail used a long knife to slice strips off a big lump of fatty meat that turned round and round on a spit. He made us what are called Kebabs and tucked them into cardboard packets and said Enjoy! they're juicy and full of flavour. I told him they were more like bits of old roof felt, and he arched his eyebrows which were even bigger than the caterpillars in David Attenborough programmes. Fat ran down my arms and turned hard. It was like wearing gloves and I had to scrape it off.

Give him a kebab cut, Bernhard told Ismail. Ismail said I'd have to wait till he'd finished serving his customers, then he'd take the meat off the spit and sit me on it instead. And I'd go round and round and he'd slice off my hair.

Bernhard began lifting me up on the spit and said Right, Ismail, let's do it, and Sally punched him.

I told Ismail he shouldn't mix kebabs and haircutting, it's unhealthy and against the law. If he did men with clipboards would come round and make him shut his shop and he'd be deported back to Turkey. Ismail looked worried, so we left.

Back at Sally's Bernhard gave me what he called a Number One with a razor. It made me look very old and like the Wanted Man I am today. Bernhard said I wouldn't get a visa for this country with the new haircut because I looked like a terrorist. I told him I'd report him to the government because he's German and he was being cruel like in the War.

I haven't written any more poems. I'd like to sell the three I've written but three's not enough to make up what's called an Anthology. And two of those are only five lines long so I'd need very small pages and very big letters to make them stretch. I think I'm an Inspirational Poet, which means I write a poem when it appears in my head. Unfortunately, another hasn't yet, but it's no crisis.

Maybe I'm too CALM. Zen monks don't write much poetry because poems are usually about sad things. And as Zen monks experience Eternal Peace they're hardly ever sad or gloomy.

Nor am I, my life's too interesting. Monks don't have lady friends either, especially those with no clothes on, because they live in small cells on their own and pray all day and never go to parties or discos to meet any. So they don't write poems about love. I don't either, even though I love Sally.

I've decided that being a poet is much too much hard work.

First you have to wait for inspiration.

Then you write the poems.

Then get them printed in a book.

Then sell your book to booksellers.

Then they have to sell it to hundreds of customers before you get any money.

Which could take quite a long time.

I've decided to be an artist instead. I've been to another jumble sale and bought a book of paintings by a man called Picasso. You see his name on cars so I think he was French. I bought a beret, too, and a dress like Mr or Mrs Rawson's smock so I look like a proper artist.

I think being an artist will be a lot easier than being a poet. I'll paint a painting, sell it to someone, and get paid hundreds of pounds straightaway.

How to start? I'm using my toothbrush as a paint brush. And I've mixed mango squash and mud with berries and bits of bark and water from a puddle to make paints. I'll be the first organic painter and help combat the World Climate Crisis. People like vegetarian food so they'll probably like my vegetarian pictures.

I've been thinking. Painting things exactly as they are in real life is difficult when you're a beginner. Trees have to look like trees and houses like houses. If they don't people think you're not very good and won't buy.

Mr Picasso was what they call an Abstract Artist. An intriguing word. I've looked it up in my dictionary and it says 'relating to or denoting art that does not attempt to represent external reality but rather seeks to achieve its effect using shapes, colours and textures'. I'm not sure what that means, but it can't be difficult as his paintings look a bit of a mess.

I've been looking through Mr Picasso's book and I'm puzzled. Why did he pick ugly ladies to paint? I'd paint Sally if she was here, she's lovely. I'd be surprised if Mr Picasso sold many pictures. Who wants a painting of a lady with her eyes on top of each other and a nose where her mouth should be? His ladies look like people in mirrors at the fair. When I went to the fair with Sally and Bernhard, Bernhard said the curvy mirror made me look normal.

Mr Picasso also paints pictures of crooked tables and jugs and cups and plates. He must have painted quickly, because his cups and plates would have slid off the table. I think I'll be successful because even before I've started I can paint better pictures than him.

It's not yet Twix time and I've painted four pictures already. I've painted an old mill by a river. Abstract painters make everything look like what it isn't so I've left the mill out. Which I think is intriguing. In another picture I've painted the mill upside down, and in another made it look like a bungalow. Why not? Who set External Reality in stone?

My last picture was even easier and took me three minutes. I painted everything black. It shows the mill at night when you can't see it at all, and nothing else either.

I like being a painter and I think I'm already quite good.

I've put my easel up near the toilet in a lay by so when people stop to do a number one or number two they can watch me paint. It smells a bit by the toilet, but it's no hardship.

Works of art must do what they call Speak for Themselves so I won't answer questions about what this bit of the painting is or what that bit means. I've written the prices in big letters people can see from the road.

A man and a lady stop for a pee. She's even uglier than

Mr Picasso's ladies. I ask the man Can I paint your wife?

The man says We're in a bit of a hurry.

She says I'd love to be painted, Donald.

I tell them Don't worry, it won't take long, I'm an Abstract Artist.

It's my first commission. I'll make it very Abstract to play safe. I paint the lady with one eye bigger than the other, ears that stick out, an upside down nose, and green hair. I think it's one of my best, but when I show it to the lady she starts to cry.

Do I really look like that, Donald?

The man hugs her and says Don't worry, darling, you don't.

It's important that they buy the painting because it's of one lady in particular and no one else. Painters have to be good salesmen so I tell her she's not as ugly in External Reality as she looks in the painting, and she cries even more.

They don't buy it. Which is curious.

Most humans are ugly. They can be fat, spotty, have a big nose, or a pot belly. It makes me think hard about how to paint pictures of ugly people and still sell them. It's important I think of an answer.

Sally isn't ugly, she's lovely. If I painted her nose where her chin is and her eyes where her ears are, she'd still be.

I think Mr Picasso must have made lots of ugly ladies cry when they saw his paintings. Maybe he was cruel. A lot of French people were and probably still are. They killed other French people they didn't like with a giant blade that crashed down and cut their necks, and everyone cheered when their heads fell into a basket.

Painting a face in a picture is not like assembling Billy,

Nils and Nita together. There are no instructions and I put all the bits of face together exactly how I want. Which I think is what Mr Picasso must have done.

It's lunchtime. I haven't sold any paintings yet but it is summer, so it's light much longer till it gets dark, and people will still have to stop to pee on their way home. Lots are going to the toilet. One man does his pee then stops and says That's interesting, I'll buy that. It'll remind me of my estranged wife, the bitch.

It's the picture of the ugly lady who cried.

I'm wondering if it's best if I paint other men's wives and sell them to other wives' husbands. Maybe that's what Mr Picasso did.

I haven't sold any more pictures. I've decided that painting ladies is just as difficult as writing poems. Ladies care too much how they look. Sally does. Which is why they spend so much time in the bathroom with bottles and tubes and Miracle Hair Insurance and Body Butter and have wardrobes as big as my hut.

I think I'll specialize in painting men. Men don't mind having their eyes in the wrong place or their noses where their chins should be. Maybe I've discovered what they call a Gap in the Market.

I tell one man my painting of him doesn't attempt to represent External Reality but rather seeks to achieve its effect using shape, colour and texture.

He says, Very interesting, I'll buy it.

I'm tired from all the painting. I need to find a bed

and breakfast. Down a lane near the sea I see an old house like a castle. It's got battlements and a big black door with wavy iron hinges. It doesn't have a friendly face and there's a NO VACANCIES sign.

I don't knock because there's no knocker. A wire says Pull.

I pull and nothing happens.

I pull and nothing happens.

I pull and nothing happens.

It'll be morning soon and I won't need a B&B.

At last the door creaks and a man wearing a striped dressing gown peeps out and says Looking for accommodation, young man? Come in, welcome to Draycott Manor.

I say But your sign says NO VACANCIES.

We are indeed closed for restoration, but you might as well stay now you're here.

He calls out Alice! We've a young man wanting accommodation.

A lady in a purple nightie with a plastic bag on her head comes down the stairs and says We're closed for restoration, but you might as well stay now you're here. It's just £70 for a single. We'll show you your room. This way.

It's darker inside this house than it is outside. Even badgers and bats would be bumping into each other. There's just one light bulb and it's not working.

The rooms have got carpets on the walls but not on the floor, which is curious, and the stairs are guarded by knights in armour. They're fierce and look as if they mean me no good. I lift up the visor of one and look inside.

'No one at home', I say, but Mr Harold and Mrs Alice

don't laugh.

We climb the stairs, go along a corridor, up more stairs, along another corridor, and up more stairs.

I ask where the fire doors are like in the Minehead B&B. The man says Draycott Manor is a Historical Property and we're not allowed any. I tell him old buildings catch fire and burn down and I won't feel safe without fire doors. I also ask Mr Harold if they've got snakes in the pipes but he's not listening. He pushes open a creaking door.

Here's your room, young man. As you see, superior guest accommodation in a unique historical setting. We think Henry the Eighth stayed here.

And it comes with an authentic Tudor four-poster bed reputedly slept in by Queen Bess, says Mrs Alice. She presses the mattress and historical dust flies into the air.

The room looks old and mouldy to me and Queen Bess can't have had much of a night's sleep. I spot a stain on the wall above the bed and say I don't think that damp stain's very superior.

You're wrong there, says Mrs Alice and smiles at Mr Harold and he smiles back.

I paid thirty pounds not seventy in Minehead for my B&B and there wasn't any damp. And it had fire doors.

It's actually not a damp stain, says Mr Harold, it's a wall painting.

I tell them If that's a painting it's even more abstract than Mr Picasso's. It may be on the wall, but I don't think it's a painting at all, it's a damp stain. I'm an artist and I know a painting when I see one. And why a painting on the wall? If you wanted to sell it you'd have to sell the house as well.

Young man, says Mr Harold, Draycott Manor is a noted historic building and we're fortunate to have a wealth of medieval wall paintings of national importance gracing our rooms.

Including an exceptional Doom in the Master, says Mrs Alice.

I touch the stain with my fingers. That's damp, I tell them. I know all about damp because the roof leaks in my hut and water's coming up through the floor.

Actually it's conservation in progress, says Mrs Alice. We've had the V&A down for the one in the Master.

Mr Harold nods. And this is our Margaret of Antioch. That's her there.

Did she pay £70 to stay in this damp old room?

Margaret's medieval, he says. This wall painting depicts her martyrdom. See that faint shape there? That's her being scourged with knives and pincers. And that wheel's the rack she was tortured on. It's of national significance.

And unique quality of detail, says Mrs Alice.

I don't think so, I'm thinking. For £70 this room looks second-rate, if not third or fourth. I'm having what are called Second Thoughts and I'm not sure I want to stay in a room where a lady's being tortured, even if it did happen a long time ago. I tell them I'll find somewhere else.

If you do you'll be turning down a unique opportunity to experience period accommodation in a historic building of national importance, says Mr Harold.

And you can have the room for fifty pounds, says Mrs Alice.

Never turn down a bargain, son, dad told me.

Okay, I say.

I can't sleep. Which is good news because I won't have to worry about waking up in time for breakfast. But I keep thinking about poor Margaret being tortured above my head. Ken the plastic iguana keeps falling off the bed head and snuggling up to me so he's not happy either.

It's dark in this room, darker than the combe at night. And I'm still choking on all the dust on the carpet that Mr Harold probably isn't allowed to sweep up because it's historic. Even the shadows have shadows. I can hear footsteps outside, and creakings and rustlings. The walls are making noises which I hope is water gurgling through historic pipes and not wriggling snakes. I hope they don't leak till after I've left tomorrow. Which is now today.

At the Minehead B&B there was Electricity running through wires in the walls, but I don't think so here because there's just one light bulb and it's in the ceiling. Which looks historical too, as plaster keeps falling on my head. I'm not surprised I'm the only guest when the rooms have got paintings of doom and gloom and people being tortured. If I was on holiday I'd want happy pictures on the walls.

I've been thinking hard. These two old people have got what's called a Business in Decline. I'm an artist, and I'd like to help them get more customers for their historic B&B. I don't believe they're not allowed to replace the pipes or hoover up the dust or get fire doors so guests don't get burned alive. I think they haven't done it because they haven't got any money. If they had money they could afford to make their historical house modern and buy a hoover and more light bulbs. Henry the Eighth

144

might have enjoyed staying here in what are called the Olden Days, but in his time the house would have been new and modern, with serfs to sweep up the dust which was new dust then and not historic. And flaming torches instead of bulbs which hadn't been invented.

I put on my beret and smock and get out my paints. I'll turn the damp stain into a mural, like the one on the bus station wall at home. Margaret's face is faded and I can't tell whether she's ugly or not. I think Sally would look nicer, so I paint her face on Margaret because Sally's is the face I'd like to wake up to. I put Margaret's ears or nose in the right places for once and give her Sally's smile exactly where her mouth should be.

People like fun fairs when they're on holiday at the seaside, so I turn the wheel Margaret's being tortured on into a big wheel like you see at the fair, and paint tiny families enjoying a ride on it. I like crashing into people on dodgems, so I paint some of them, and fairy lights and stalls where you shoot corks through rifles, and hook plastic ducks, and throw darts at playing cards.

It took me till breakfast time and I'm very tired.

When I open the curtains and the sun shines in through the historic dust I inspect the great job I've done. I'll take a photo of it on my mobile to show to customers. I'm glad I've bothered to help Mr Harold and Mrs Alice. They'll get more guests and be prosperous and happy in the Evening of Their Lives.

At breakfast I tell them the good news. I suggest I could paint over all the other wall paintings in their historic house if they wanted, and make Draycott Manor a friendly, modern, up-to-date B&B.

Mr Harold chokes on his cornflakes, falls over, and bangs his head on the Aga and Mrs Harold screams. They run up the stairs, shrieking. It's great, they're even more pleased with my idea than I thought.

I eat my cornflakes and burnt toast. Mr Harold runs back into the room poking what's called a Pike at me that knights killed each other with.

What have you done, you little idiot? You've destroyed our wall painting! We're ruined! Alice, phone the police!

Time to go. I grab my rucksack, easel and paints and rush out of the door and down the lane before I get tortured like Margaret from Antioch. Some people will never learn how to run a successful business. It takes all sorts.

I'm a Wanted Man for two crimes now.

I'm painting in a lay by miles down the road from Draycott Manor. Rumble noises up the road. Black smoke. A motorbike and sidecar. It's black and old and it rattles, and bumps up onto the verge and I jump out of the way.

The rider takes off his goggles. You again, my limping twin. Well, what have we here?

I tell him I haven't written enough poems to be a poet, so now I'm an Abstract Artist.

Ground-breaking, he says. The shock of the new. Jasper Johns, look at this one!

It's an ugly woman, I tell him. One of a series I'm calling Ladies in Lay Bys.

Ugly? She's ravishing! Her internal beauty transcends the strictures of gender. She's an exquisite creature – the dark mons pubis replacing the mouth and lips. A dominatrix par excellence, striking terror and desire into man, beckoning him towards sensual ecstasy. And what have we here – ah, landscapes. Curiously, they possess or paradoxically fail to possess an absence of subject matter. Colour, form and texture dance across the canvas, conjuring a thrilling alignment of microcosm and macrocosm. And my God, look at this! A mill or lack of mill, an emptiness disclosing a dark portal beckoning us towards immeasurable space. A thrilling inversion that restructures disparate elements, hovering enticingly between the abstract and the representational.

You like them? I ask.

Like 'em? I love 'em. What media are you using? Your work possesses a transparent luminosity. Acrylics?

I'm confused. I thought Acrylics were what we did in the gym at school, but I think he means paints. I tell him I mixed mango squash and mud from the verge with berries and bits of bark, and water from a puddle.

Worryingly fugitive, he says and looks doubtful. We'll need to sell them quick before they fade. You need an agent. Luckily I'm one of the best. As it's you I'll accept just the standard seventy percent commission. Quick, load them in the sidecar, I'll take them to Rawson's. I'll have to work fast, I need my commission post haste.

The motorbike races off and Mr Hardaker's gone. I'm on the verge choking on smoke. I've got an agent but no paintings.

I get a lift from a man who writes newspapers.

Any scandal? he asks. Heard about any celebrities shagging other celebrities' wives? Vicars doing unpleasant things with minors? Bodies buried in gardens? I've fifty column inches to fill by five.

He drops me at Helen's home, gives me a card, nods at the home, and says Let me know about any abuses in there you hear about, and roars off.

I've come to visit Helen, I tell the nurse who opens the door.

Which Helen's that? We've two.

Helen who lost her book.

Her surname is?

Helen Jacobs.

You're family?

I want to give Helen her book back.

She's allowed family visits only, I'm afraid.

It's important, she'll want it back. She said If you find this book return it to Helen Jacobs, 33 Riverside Close, Budleigh Salterton. And in red ink. But she doesn't live there any more. It's about hamsters.

Ah, hamsters. The nurse looks worried. Best not give it to her.

I can't give it to her, I've left it in Derek's van.

The nurse sighs. In that case, wait here.

I'm waiting. I smell greens and cauliflower. And toilets like at mum and dad's home. An old lady on crutches nudges me and says Sssh, don't tell anyone, and taps the side of her nose.

I won't, I reply.

I can't, I don't know what it is. Her pockets are stuffed with paper hankies and she's got coloured curlers in her hair like a Christmas tree.

The nurse comes back and says You can see Helen.

For a few minutes. But, please, whatever you do, don't mention hamsters.

We go down a corridor, along another one, up some stairs and along another. I smell more cauliflower. We go into room number 26.

Hello, Helen, I say. I've come to return your book. But I can't because Derek's got it in his van and you aren't allowed it anyway.

Helen's got ginger hair. She's quite pretty and what they call Pleasantly Plump. She's wearing long black boots and driving a red electric scooter very fast round the room. It's like the scooter the old man next door had who ran over our cat Megan then who got run over himself by a lorry. Dad said it was what they call Poetic Justice.

Helen crashes into me, and I tell her she needs four-piston monobloc aluminium caliper brakes.

Are you French? she asks.

Non, I say. Which I think is almost a joke, but a French one.

A shame, she says. I like the French, they like snails. I do too. Especially Helix pomatia. I'm on hunger strike till they give me some.

I tell her Mum and dad get chops and chicken in their Home.

I don't want to eat them, stupid, I want to race them. I've no source of supply here. This building's too well insulated for snails to get in. It's like a sealed tomb with people waiting to die. I found an Arianta arbustorum behind the wardrobe once and matron called in the Environmental Department. I hid it and keep it in my old tooth mug in case another turns up. You need two to race.

I like your hair, I tell her. Our neighbour's cat had ginger hair but it died.

I'm dying, too, so the doctor says. He's got bad breath and looks up my skirt and won't show me what he's writing in my notes.

We'd better get your book back from Derek quick then so you've got time to read it. But Derek's never where he's meant to be because of his satnav lady.

What book's that?

Your hamster book. Oh, I forgot, I wasn't supposed to mention it.

Helen's eyes grow large, then larger still. She's turning redder and redder and panting. I hope she's not having a fit. I'm worried, I definitely shouldn't have mentioned hamsters. I'm about to run to the door to call for the nurse when Helen says Sod the hamsters. I've moved on. You like scootering? Jump on the back.

We're doing laps round the room, faster and faster. We've broken the Sound Barrier and Helen says we've reached Australia and we should look out for wallabies. I'm giddy from bumping into the wardrobe.

We skid to a stop. Helen's whispering.

Help me escape, she says. Then we'll find Derek. I don't remember the book but I might want it back when I see it. It's a shame it's about hamsters and not snails. I like snails more now. I think they must have given me some sort of anti-hamster drug here. All I've got now is a furry hamster called Reg they don't know about. He's not real.

I tell her I've got a plastic iguana called Ken who rides on the front of Lars my bike. Or he did till Lars got stolen by a Gentleman of the Road.

Surely the nurses won't let you escape, Helen, I say.

Homes are just prisons without bars on the windows. Mum and dad can't escape. The old people all wear striped pyjamas that make them look like prisoners. Dad tried to escape once when mum watched too many Daytime Reality Programmes on the telly. He tripped over his dressing gown in the main road and caused a road traffic accident. He was on the news.

We'll wait till dinner time then escape, says Helen. The nurses will be feeding the patients chops and cabbage and stewed apples and custard because it's Wednesday and they'll be too busy to see us. You can hide in the wardrobe till then. When matron comes round I'll tell her you've already left. She's bound to want to check just in case you're a terrorist.

She won't think that, Helen, I reassure her. Terrorists blow the building down with explosives and rush in and shoot everyone with machine guns. I knocked politely and came in through the front door and signed what the nurse called the Register.

Helen's wardrobe's more comfortable than mum and dad's at home which had mum's shoes all over the floor. The high heeled shoes she wore for British Legion dances pierced my bottom once and I had to go to A&E. Helen's dresses and brassieres are dangling down from the rail and making me sneeze, but it's no crisis.

This wardrobe's too small to lie down in and not tall enough to stand up in, so I'm sitting in the special yoga Lotus position Sally showed me. She sits in it for hours and wears a leotard. It's pink and very tight. Once I screwed up my eyes and it looked like she was nude. I tried hard not to peek but I did have an Urge.

Urges are irresistible.

I've got cramp, which was not mentioned in the yoga guide Sally lent me.

Helen's given me a book to read but it's too dark to see it.

I'm still inside the wardrobe and thinking hard about books. In the dark all books look the same, which is intriguing. And they feel the same when you touch them because they've all got covers and pages. A book in the dark could be by Mr Shakespeare or Wordworth the poet, or it could be telling you how to repair washing machines. I'm feeling the covers of Helen's book and rubbing my fingers over the words on the pages like a blind person, but I've still no idea what it's about. I'll just have to wait. I hope it's not about hamsters.

After an hour I've got very bad cramp. I hear a knock on the door and matron comes in.

Where's your visitor? she asks.

Gone.

Has he? He didn't sign out.

Who cares.

I do, Helen. No need to speak like that. He should have told us.

Search the wardrobe if you like, you won't find him.

I'm about to scream with cramp. If I do I'll be discovered.

Then I do scream, but I do it Soundlessly, which is what people in horror films do when they see the door handle turning and the murderer about to come in to kill them. Which is exactly what matron is about to do to me.

The rules about visitors are to protect you, Helen.

I'm fed up to the teeth with your bloody rules. I've a good mind to escape. Go on, search the wardrobe if you must, I don't give a damn.

I think we'll be asking the doctor to up your medication if you go on like this, my girl.

The door slams.

Helen throws open the wardrobe doors and I fall on the floor locked in what's called the Foetal Position. I can't move my legs and I'm still holding Helen's book. At last I can look at the cover. It's called Advanced Ducting Solutions for Mechanical Engineers Volume 3.

Quick, come on, says Helen. They're serving dinner, time to go. Pass me my coat. And that scarf. And fill this plastic bag with the stuff in the drawer. Make sure you put my fags and lighter and my rabbit in.

I collect it all up and stuff it in the bag. Curious, her rabbit doesn't look much like a rabbit at all, more like the policeman's baton but a bit smaller. Maybe Helen uses it to ward off rude men.

I'll wear my dark glasses, she says, the nurses won't recognise me. You can wear my sun hat, it'll hide your face. You'll look a bit like a Cornu aspersum, the nurses won't be watching for escaping snails.

We're in disguise. Only we know who we are, and I wouldn't recognize us. It's intriguing being someone else.

Anything's better than being stuck in this home, says Helen. Come on, we'll scoot down the corridor and escape through the front door.

We use the lift. I press the buttons one by one and we go up and down three times. I like lifts. Then as we scoot down the corridor the old lady on crutches whispers Sssh, don't tell anyone, young man, and taps the side of her nose again as we race by. I whisper back I didn't and won't, and tap the side of my nose. There are no nurses anywhere and we're out through the front door.

I balance on the back as we scoot along the main road towards my hut, wherever that is. There's no satnav on Helen's scooter to tell us the way, and she doesn't stop at traffic lights, even when they're red.

No time, she shouts back, imagine they're green.

Which they are after we've passed. What's a red light when you're criminals on the run?

We're through the town and out in the country.

We'll go to my hut, I say. They won't find you there. Or me, I'm a Wanted Man. And you're a Wanted Woman.

That's exactly what I want to be before I die, says Helen. Wanted by men, as many as possible. You don't wear a string vest, do you? she says. They're a sexual turn off.

We've scooted miles.

I'm tired, let's stop here and race some snails, Helen says. We had to play Scrabble and other stupid games in the afternoons at the home. I got bored. I kept winning with words like Muzjiks, Zuz, and Xylyl. The off-duty doctors played sometimes, and I'd wind them up by putting down words like Oxyphenbutazone. When I got challenged by the other players I told them it's a non-steroidal anti-inflammatory drug, and why didn't they know that, as half of them were swallowing it three times day. I wanted to hold snail races in the long corridor, but when I showed them a Monacha cantiana I'd found in the rose bushes three patients fainted and matron called in Rentakil. Come on, let's find some snails and have a race.

Look out for Cornu aspersums, they're fast.

I'm searching the hedge for snails. I find a big one and a small one and some empty shells with no snails in.

I'll have that big Monacha cantiana, says Helen. We'll give your smaller Hygromia cinctella a handicap start. They're slow like me. I've got a handicap.

I whistle and they're off.

Except they're not. My snail goes one way and Helen's the other. I turn mine round and it goes back into its shell and stays there.

These snails are not breaking the Sound Barrier.

Half an hour passes.

Mine's won, says Helen.

We didn't agree where the winning post is, I say.

Just there, says Helen, where mine is. Come on, let's have another race.

Hours later, the snails are still racing. They haven't gone far, and mine's back where it started.

We really need racing snails like Cornu aspersums, Helen says. They reach incredible speeds of three feet an hour. Let's look for some.

I'm too tired, I tell her.

Me too, says Helen, then drives her scooter over the snails and scrunches them.

I thought you liked snails.

Not those slowcoaches, she says. Come on, let's get going.

We're racing through the country again, past cottages and churches and fields and woods and farms. At last we reach a hay barn.

We'll stay here for the night, I say.

We won't, I've got standards, says Helen, I don't slum.

But we do stay because it's late. I make two hay beds. Not a double, that would be taking advantage of a lady and not polite, as we've only just met.

Helen smokes a cigarette and tosses the end in the hay. It makes a handy fire and we warm our hands. I put the flames out just before it burns the barn down.

I'm on the run from the police, I tell her. I had a gun.

Did you shoot someone?

No.

Shame, I know plenty of candidates, especially that damn matron.

The police took the gun.

That's a shame too, says Helen. Was it a Glock 19? I hope so. It offers superior fire power and guarantees a high degree of kill accuracy. I particularly like its modular back strap system so the shooter can instantly customise the grip. If I was a shooter I'd use one. It's useful for girl assassins with a small hand size, isn't it?

How should I know? How does she?

In the morning we're hungry and we've no food so we eat our dream breakfasts.

Mine's sugar snapcrackles, which is actually the same as my real breakfast. Helen hated the krispies and cold scrambled egg she got in the home and breakfasts on what she calls arugula and pistachio pesto quiche, then shakshouka and mint tea.

You probably haven't noticed, says Helen. I've got attractive legs but they don't work. That's why I use crutches. My legs aren't proper legs, really, because they won't walk.

I like your soldiers' boots.

Steel-tipped weapons. When you're sexually attractive like me you need to be particular about what men you entice. I asked the doctors if I could have new legs like people get new hands or hearts, but they said no. I got so fed up I told them horses' legs would do. They'd be hidden under my skirt so no one could tell. They thought I was serious, no sense of humour.

You could run in the Grand National if you had horses' legs. Do you talk to your legs like I talk to Billy, Nils and Nita?

I keep telling them it's in their interests – and mine – to walk but they won't.

You could join a circus and walk on your hands, you don't need legs for that.

An intriguing prospect I will give thought to. God I was bored in the home! It was a nun's life. I want to travel before I die. Explore the Arctic, go inside a volcano, visit the Temple of Rats.

You could be a mermaid, they don't need legs, they've got a flipper.

Helen's thinking. Hmm, another interesting idea. If I try hard I could probably grow one quite quickly. It's what's called Accelerated Evolution, a concept pioneered by the Frenchman Lamarck. But on reflection it wouldn't be a good idea to be a mermaid as I'd get caught in a fisherman's net and be gutted and made into fish fingers. But on second reflection that's probably better than living in that damn home.

You'll like my hut, I tell her. It's perfect for people with legs that don't work, there's no upstairs.

We forgot to bring Helen's crutches when we escaped so she can't walk. We're scooting along the middle of the main road because we don't want to get stuck in drains. Helens says we're Commanding the Road.

We're not breaking the sound barrier because Helen says her scooter's a toy one for indoors. It goes ten miles very slowly then stops. She says she wants the All Terrain GX246 model, with a 3-phase AC powered motor, a GIVI Trekker storage box, a 75 AH battery with a 40 mile range, 3-mode power, high torque, anti-tip puncture proof wheels, adjustable speed control, and an integrated braking system and a delta tiller bar.

Twix time. Helen says she's enjoyed lots of men in her time. Whatever time that was and whatever it means. Her legs don't work but everything else does, she says. She asks me if I've enjoyed lots of women. I tell her I enjoy Sally. She says as she's dying she wants to be as Promiscuous as possible. I need my dictionary.

We're scooting again and making a long train behind us. A supermarket lorry's hooting and the driver shouts and waves his fist. I call out We're Commanding the Road and can't go any faster because we haven't got a 75 AH battery with 3-mode power but he's not listening, just swearing like Derek. He swerves into us and almost knocks me off and Helen shouts at him to Fuck off, and hopes he won't reach the supermarket before it closes and the dead pigs inside his lorry will go rotten and cause a Health Hazard and he'll lose his job. His lorry blows smoke at us, but we're electric so we can't blow any back.

Then we come to a sudden stop and roll back down

the hill. Helen yells that the scooter battery's run out and needs recharging. It's intriguing, there's loads of electricity in the countryside but it's locked up in pylons so you can't use it. Pylons are buzzing everywhere, fizzing with electricity, but there are no plugs to plug the scooter battery in.

I tell Helen her scooter's now an Immobility Scooter, but she doesn't laugh. I thought it was a good joke.

There's a long train behind us and we've stopped Commanding the Road, and they're all hooting and shouting and swearing. Helen tells me to give the scooter a kick. I do, then give it a good talking to like I do Billy, Nils and Nita. I give the battery the end of my tongue, too, but that doesn't work either. So I push the scooter to the top of the hill into a lay by and all the cars race by hooting and shouting

I need crutches, says Helen, and quick.

I push the scooter for hours with Helen sitting on it till we get to a village and find a surgery.

It's full of patients with gloomy faces. They're sitting on chairs round the walls reading magazines about gardening, weddings and cake icing. They've got broken arms and spots and swollen legs, and are sniffing and coughing. I poke toilet paper up my nose – you can't be too careful, a surgery's not a healthy place. Aunt Beryl visited her doctor every day for a year and still died. She became a Medical Mystery. Dad said the doctor got fed up with seeing her and probably gave her poison pills to get rid of her.

An old man in the corner has fallen off his chair. He looks dead but everyone else is too ill to notice. The lady at reception slides back a window and says Yes?

I tell her a lady outside needs crutches.

No problem, wait here, she says.

Being healthy when everyone else is ill is not polite, so while I wait I do some coughing and sneezing to fit in.

She comes back with crutches. Does the person want any help? she asks.

No thank you, I say.

I go back out and give Helen the crutches.

She clunks round the car park trying them out. How much were they?

The lady didn't ask for any money, I tell her. Come on .

I'm pushing the scooter while Helen walks on the crutches. We turn on to a small road then on to a smaller one, then into a lane. Round a corner we see a Road Closed sign.

Better turn round, says Helen.

I don't think so, I tell her. This is just where Derek could be. His satnav lady likes dead ends.

In the distance mud's flying in a field.

And there's a van with Actuating Logistics Solutions Countrywide painted on the side.

That's Derek, I say.

His van is churning mud and hurling it into the sky. He's trying to go backwards. Cows are helping, they're nudging the van and poking their heads through the windows giving advice.

I poke my head through the other window and say Hello, Derek. It's me, you've got Helen's book. He tells me to Fuck off.

I tell him cows are clever at getting out of fields, so it would be in his interest to let them help. But Derek's not listening, just swearing at his satnav lady.

I'm looking at the number the cows' bottoms makes. I don't think it's a phone number. Helen says it's the distance between Peru and Nicaragua. Also the number of oil filters exported by Belgium. Helen's clever.

Derek stops swearing, looks at his list and says he's already delivered Helen's book to 33 Riverside Close, Budleigh Salterton, so we can't bloody well have it back.

But Helen doesn't live there any more, I tell him, and she doesn't live at the home either. He gets cross and says Fucking typical. Whatever I do turns out wrong and for two pins I'd chuck the whole fucking job in and become a male model. I've got gym membership and I'm gelling and building a six pack.

Helen tells him not to bother as she doesn't fancy enjoying him at all.

We're off.

I've been pushing the scooter for miles and I'm at the End of what dad called His Tether, but in this case Mine. Dad was always at the end of his when we had Sunday lunch at Aunt Megs' house. He didn't like her fatty roast beef and soggy dumplings, or listening to her moaning about the cat next door that kept pooing on her geraniums.

Helen says my scooter pushing is even slower than a Cornu aspersum snail, which is very slow indeed. She keeps shouting Push harder, and already she's miles ahead out of sight on her crutches.

At last I catch her up, but I'm puffed. She's watching

swallows dive bombing a field. They're catching flies in their beaks.

We're going to need money, Helen says.

I tell her I don't think my pin number will keep working for much longer. We'll have to find jobs. Maybe I can bring some more dead plants back to life at a garden centre.

No one will employ me, she says. Most jobs need legs and mine don't work, so my career prospects are practically nil. What can you do?

I tell her I'm a poet, comedian, entertainer and trainee psychiatrist. And I want to be a TV celebrity.

A shade unfocused, she says, you need Career Advice. Entertaining sounds the best bet. I've thought of one thing we could do. Train swallows to be Red Arrows and charge people to watch.

I'm excited. We'll add them to my act, I say. I'll be famous and mum and dad can watch me on daytime telly. If they're still alive, which I hope they will be. Poor mum and dad.

Helen says We'll learn swallow language so we can tell the birds what formations to make so it's an exciting show. It'll be easier than making them learn English.

We agree sign language might be best. We can wave flags like Admirals when they signal to the fleet.

Let's start straightaway, I say.

We've thought of a problem. Red Arrow swallows can only be a summer act because they fly south in winter. They get an Urge, and Urges, as I know, are difficult to resist. When my bottom says Scratch me, I scratch it, even in company. Zen monks don't get Urges. They never feel the Urge to go anywhere. They stay in one place, even if they've got a thorn poking up their backside.

I've thought of one good thing. Swallows come back to the same place every spring, so we won't need to go far to catch them.

But we still won't make any money in winter, says Helen. And I like expensive things. People who are dying do.

I think hard. I tell her they won't have to be just a summer act if we keep them in a warm cage in winter with palm leaves and a coconut. You can wear a grass skirt and me a sombrero, so the swallows will think they're in the Tropics. They must have very small brains so they'll think they've migrated. We'll tow the cage behind the scooter and open the door and let them fly out and perform aerial displays.

Helen says they may be unhappy being stuck in a cage all winter when they should have flown south. They'll probably refuse to be Red Arrows and just want to propagate with female swallows and build nests and catch flies. Not very exciting as an act.

I suggest we could use geese. Geese stay here in the winter. They think our cold is warm, because they come all the way from the Arctic which is colder than the inside of mum's freezer. We wouldn't have to train them at all, as geese are already Red Arrows and fly in interesting V shapes without being told to.

At Twix time we decide geese wouldn't make good Red Arrows, either, because they fly almost as high as the real Red Arrows, and they honk and make lots of noise and wouldn't hear us telling them what formations to make. And they'd just be tiny specks and not much of a spectacle for the audience down below.

Bats fly, Helen says.

They do, I say, but the bats only come out at night, which is not very helpful for afternoon matinées.

We wonder whether sheep could be Red Arrows, but they'd have to be Red Arrows on the ground as they don't fly. We'd need a dog to make them run in V shapes. But I say we have to be sensible about these things, sheep are stupid,. Helen says the best thing you can do with sheep is make them into cutlets.

Helen's tired so I'm carrying her.

We go a hundred yards, then I go back to the scooter, push it and catch up.

We go a hundred yards then I go back to the scooter, push it and catch up.

We go a hundred yards then I go back to the scooter, push it and catch up.

I think we're getting there, but I've no idea where there is.

It's dark and I'm walking slower and slower. Dark is dangerous, we could fall down a hole any minute. Planets fall down holes called Black Holes. They're attracted to them by an irresistible Urge that's something to do with Gravity.

Helen says black holes are actually regions of space-time exhibiting extreme gravitational effects that not even electromagnetic radiation can escape.

We've no torch and it's too late to find a campsite. I

like the dark. My hut gets dark at night, but it's no crisis because I know where everything is. When I'm outside at night I know if I walk one and a bit steps past the holly I'll poke my eye out on the thorn, and I know I have to jump to miss the old mangle sticking out of the ground behind the hut.

Helen tells me she prefers the sun which she says is actually a G-type main-sequence star composed of hot plasma with internal convective motion generating a magnetic field via a dynamo process, and converting millions of tons of inert matter into energy every second. It activates Life on Earth, combining chlorophyll with carbon dioxide to generate plant growth.

Helen's clever. I tell her the sun wasn't much help at the Garden centre. It dried up lots of plants and they almost died, and I had to water them to bring them back to life.

So you were a sort of God, Helen said.

I'm talking about something I've been thinking about a lot. What did God see after He made light? Lots of stuff He didn't know was there before? Or did God make all the stuff in the Universe because when He invented light there was nothing to see?

Helen thinks God was probably lonely before He invented light.

I point out that he must have been just as lonely after He invented light because He made rocks for millions of years after, and rocks are not great companions and don't say much at all.

We're staying in another barn and sharing Random Thoughts.

It's got holes in the roof and tin sides that bang in the wind. Helen's keeping a look out for rats while I'm staring up at the stars. Sometimes I think stars are friendly, I tell her, but I'm not really sure. They could be shooting poison rays at us. That's why I prefer sleeping indoors at night, you can't be too careful.

Helen tells me that intellectually I'm a bit of a Neanderthal, which I think is probably a compliment. I'll look it up. Maybe it's something to do with being an entertainer. I tell her I really want to be a Man of Mystery and go on telly. Bernhard told me I make people laugh, but not at my jokes, and Sally hit him.

I explain to Helen how I'll pull stuff out of a hat, like a pack of tiny playing cards, then a magnifying glass, then a trumpet, then a hair slide (which I'm saving for Sally), then a pair of red lips, then a moustache. And how it's important I don't pull the same things out twice because it's not so entertaining. You learn with experience.

I'll be Debbie McGhee, says Helen. I'll wear a gold bikini and smile and look desirable to the men in the audience. It'll add glamour to your act.

And I'll tell jokes while I'm performing magic and make the audience laugh. Sally said I've got a Sunny Disposition. Helen says she had one herself till the nurses made her drink a whole flask of Ribena and eat pork chops and sprouts every day.

Time to make up our beds. I drag two hay bales over and cut the string with a sharp flint. Then I toss it all over the floor to make a giant bed.

Dark clouds are covering the moon and we huddle together under the straw. I'm shivering, and I suddenly remember that we're Wanted. I tell Helen it's exciting being Wanted Criminals on the run.

We're a gang, she says.

I've just woken up. Someone's leg is covering mine. For a moment I think it's Sally, but this leg feels hairy, not like Sally's which are smooth and lovely. It must be Helen's.

I whisper Wake up, hairy Helen, and hear a curious coughing noise. I turn over and see the leg doesn't belong to Sally or Helen, it belongs to a goat. I jump up and so does the goat and it runs out of the barn bleating.

Helen says we're innocent till proved guilty, but I don't think so. Detectives do what they call Fit You Up to make sure you're guilty. They've got sales targets for catching criminals like shops selling Hoovers.

We decide we're actually helping policemen pay their mortgages. It's lucky for them there are criminals like us to catch. Otherwise they'd get sacked and couldn't pay their bills and their wives would leave them, and they'd have to steal cars and get caught and Banged Up by policemen they'd worked with before who'd say they'd become Bad Apples.

Helen says We're a Valuable Social Service.

We've stopped at a shop for Twixes. A dog the size of a mouse with lots of short legs is barking outside the shop door. Helen says they're actually not legs they're nipples. When I look more closely I think she's right. She says she's got two nipples and lifts her jumper to show me.

So have I, but I don't show her because she'll see

167

my tattoo of Aunt Megs. Sometimes when I touch my nipples I get Urges, but what they're for, how should I know. But I can't have babies and that's what nipples are for, so it's curious.

The dog whimpers like all faithful friends do when they're not happy and want to be inside shops with their owners and not outside.

Dogs are stupid, Helen says. They sit outside shops hundreds of times but never learn. They always look as if their owners have left them outside forever, even when they know they've just gone in for a pint of milk. That's why I like snails, she says. Snails don't give a damn where you've gone or if you ever come back. They're too busy going somewhere themselves, which is usually behind the skirting.

My arms have gone numb from carrying Helen. I'm tired.

I'm tired, too, she says. Too tired to carry all this stuff about in my pockets. They're bulging. I'm going to get rid of it all.

She empties her pockets and throws everything in the hedge, apart from her cigarette packet and funny shaped rabbit. I'm not throwing my rabbit away, she says. I haven't used it for a bit and I need to fit in as many orgasms as I can before I die.

I don't want to throw away any of my interesting stuff. I want more. I find a stone that looks a bit like Sally if I turn it one way. When I turn it round it doesn't. Intriguing.

Everyone's houses are full of shelves packed with things they think they needed and now don't. I tell Helen about jumble sales and how mum and dad's cupboards were full of things that weren't even on shelves any more. Plates and cups and china dolls and jugs and jewellery, all calling out I'm here, remember me!

But mum and dad had already forgotten them, and I bet they couldn't remember why they'd bought them in the first place, even before they went into the Home and were very old.

Helen agrees and says When I get a house, which has to be quick because I'm dying, I'll have empty shelves so there's nothing to remember and nothing to forget. I want to live in the present while I've got still got some.

She finds what looks like a pig's ear under some leaves. It's hard and rubbery, but as the rest of the pig's not attached to it we're not sure. I tell her I think it's a fungus.

Dogs like pigs' ears, Helen says. They're dog treats. When dogs fight each other they bite off their ears too. The nurses fed me prunes in the home that looked like pigs' ears. I dropped one down the toilet, which puzzled the nurses when they examined my stool in the morning. The doctors wrote an article about it in a magazine called The Lancet.

Rumble noises up the lane. Black smoke. A motorbike and sidecar skids towards us. It's black and rattly and bumps up on the grass. I jump out of the way to stop getting squashed and Helen falls over and one of her crutches gets bent.

It's Mr Hardaker again.

I shout Hello, Mr Hardaker, where are my paintings? But he can't hear because his motorbike's growling.

Can't hear you, old chap. Hang on, I'll take my goggles off. There, that's better.

Where are my paintings? I ask, as we cough on motorbike smoke.

I'm working hard putting together a one-man show now I'm your agent, he says.

What's your commission? asks Helen.

The normal percentage.

Thirty?

A bit more.

Forty?

A shade more.

Fifty?

A smidgin more.

Sixty?

You're not far out.

Then you're a crook and criminal like us. You can join our gang.

Love to but can't stop. He puts his goggles back on and roars up the lane.

He's gone.

So you're an artist as well as an entertainer, says Helen.

An Abstract Artist, I tell her.

You can paint me. Get your brushes out while I take my clothes off.

Helen's nude. Her legs are quite nice and look like everyone else's legs even if they don't walk. They're not hairy like the goat's, just a bit plump.

Men find me erotic, says Helen. Do you?

Helen's lying on the grass touching her nipples.

A bit fatter than Sally, I tell her. What's called Pleasurably plump.

You think about Sally a lot, don't you. Does Sally love you?

I hope so. I make her happy. I brighten her up when I go to see her. When she opens the door she says The sun's come out!

Even when it's raining.

She's your girlfriend, is she? Are you her only boyfriend?

She's got other men she does laundry for. When I go round they're in their underpants waiting for their washing to dry. Sally's kind like that. Next time I go round I'll get her to wash my trousers, but I won't show her my tattoo.

I'd like a tattoo. A Cornu aspersum crawling up my leg. They wouldn't let me have tattoos in the home in case they went septic and caused an epidemic. Show me yours.

I take my shirt off.

Ah, a map of Venezuela.

You're seeing it upside down.

Stand on your hands so I can see it properly. On second thoughts it's more like an estuarial map of the Orinoco.

Actually it's Sally, I tell her. That's what the man in the camper van said, but I think it's Aunt Megs, and she's dead.

She looks it. I'd stick to the Orinoco.

I'm painting Helen. Which feels very very rude indeed. It's like looking at the ladies without any clothes on in the magazine I found in the hedge in the combe. I hid it on Billy's top shelf. But the roof leaked and it got wet and the pages stuck together. Which was probably a good thing as it gave me Urges.

I'm glad you're an abstract artist, Helen says. Thank God you're not painting me like one of Renoir's fat women. They're boring and stupid, and not in the least erotic. I want to look erotic before I die. Sometimes in bed at the home I dreamt about being ravished, especially at night, but the doctor on the night shift had acne and smelly sweat.

I tell Helen I'm painting her using my unique Artistic Vision. All artists have one, and it's lucky for her I'm an Abstract painter, because she is a bit plump. I don't want her to cry when she sees my painting, so I'm making it Very Abstract. I've already found out that ladies care how fat or thin they look in a painting and I don't think Helen's an exception.

I paint one of her eyes poking out of her nostril and an ear sticking out of her chin. And I've painted her legs with lots of muscles like lady athletes who run marathons. She's got quite a large beard between her legs, thicker than Uncle Gilbert's. He combed his at Sunday dinner once and found a chipolata in it.

Finished at last. I show Helen my painting and tell her it doesn't attempt to represent External Reality but seeks to achieve its effect using shapes, colours and textures.

It's certainly no Renoir, she says. You could finish it off by painting a tail on my bottom like Ken the iguana's.

And I do.

I wonder if Mr Picasso felt Urges when he painted naked ladies. I had to squeeze my legs together when I was painting Helen's beard and knocked over the easel.

We've stopped in a village to buy some food. Ducks are swimming on the pond. Helen thinks they're rubber decoys.

I'm not so sure. Rubber ducks don't follow the leader like these are doing. And they're quacking, and rubber ducks don't quack unless you squeeze them.

We sit down for Twix time. Then I push Helen on the swing in the children's playground and I hang from ropes and make Tarzan noises. A mum with a ring in her nose swears at us, and a boy throws Helen's crutches in the pond. I lift my shirt and show him my tattoo of Aunt Megs and he runs off crying.

I have to wade out into the pond to get the crutches back. They look bent under water like the sticks in the stream in the combe. But they're straight when I take them out. I tell Helen you can't trust water – it bends things but doesn't. Dad was right when he warned me of the danger of Believing in Appearances. The boy who threw the crutches in the pond skims a stone at the ducks and hits one … two … three … four… five… which is quite clever. They quack and flap and fly away over the trees.

They're real or very cleverly radio-controlled decoys, Helen says.

In the village shop I pay for some food using the plastic card dad gave me to spend when it's a rainy day. It's actually warm and sunny, but Helen says it doesn't matter. I buy Twixes and cheese and bread and corned beef, cigarettes and some special tubes for Helen. They're white and furry with string poking out. The lady gives me something called Cash Back, and I take away more money from the shop than I spent. Which is even better than buying ten things for a pound in the pound shop.

I ask Helen What are the tubes for?

For my menstrual cycle, she says.

I'm quick on the uptake but I'm puzzled. Maybe her menstrual cycle's her mobility scooter. But the only tubes Lars had were inner tubes which go inside his tyres.

Poor Lars. I wonder where he is? I wouldn't trust that Gentleman of the Road to look after him properly.

We're Commanding the Road again and travelling where the road takes us. There's a long train behind us while I'm pushing Helen's mobility scooter up a long hill. Curiously there's a long train ahead of us as well, so maybe the cars and lorries in front are joining in.

When we get to the top cars are hooting and a lorry driver opens his window and shouts Fucking gyppos and throws a beer can at a gypsy with a spotted scarf and a horse that looks very Close to Death pulling a caravan.

It stops at one end of a big lay by and we stop at the other for a Twix.

We're enjoying a well earned rest.

What's that? I smell smoke and sizzling bacon. Helen's suddenly awake.

The gypsy with the spotted scarf is cooking a Full English Breakfast on a fire. His horse is tugging on a rope. It's tugging because horses always think the grass is greener where it's out of reach, even when it isn't. Just like the way so many people in this world lead sad lives Getting and Spending, which was what I think Mr

Wordworth the famous poet said in one of his poems. But he got it the wrong way round because you have to Spend before you Get. I think it's called Poetic Licence.

All except burglars, they never have to do any spending at all.

I'm glad I'm not a horse like the gypsy's, I tell Helen, even if I do live in a hut that was once a stable for Sally's neighbours' pony that died. I'd have to pull carts and put up with people sitting on my back and whipping me with a stick to make me jump fences. What's the point when all you get is a bucket of cold porridge for dinner? No thank you.

The gypsy waves to us and we jump back in the trees. I warn Helen that gypsies put curses on you and you can die. She says she wouldn't mind that much as she's dying anyway. And she's hungry and wouldn't mind a Full English Breakfast. I'm not dying and I'm not that hungry, so I hide behind a bush.

The gypsy's grinning. Welcome strangers, he shouts. Come and have a bacon sandwich.

I'm tempted, but I don't think so. Gypsies are cunning. I'm standing well back because I'm not sure how far he can cast his curse. You can't be too careful.

Have a look round my camp, he says.

We peep inside his caravan. It's dark and it's got a stove and a shelf with penguins on and shiny brass pots and photos in frames and a cupboard with mugs and plates and buckets painted with flowers.

Whole set up's a visual cliché, whispers Helen. He's not a proper gypsy. Proper gypsies are poor. They drive old camper vans with bald tyres. And this is never a proper gypsy camp. You can tell proper gypsy camps because they're surrounded by rubbish tips and rusty fridges and bits of old iron. This camp's too tidy. And he's got a MacBook Pro on the table in the van and a pin-stripe suit on a hanger and a wad of Amazon tokens in an elastic band. And he's wearing designer jeans.

Are you a proper gypsy? I ask him.

I'm a gentleman of the road, says the gypsy.

I hope not, I whisper to Helen. The last Gentleman of the Road I met stole Lars.

It's important I gain what they call the Upper Hand. Be assertive, son, that's what dad told me.

I don't want to buy any clothes pegs, I tell him. Nor does Helen. And nor does Sally, she's got a tumble dryer.

Chill, good people, says the Gentleman of the Road. So what brings you to this picturesque spot?

Picturesque? I don't think so, I'm thinking. We're in a lay-by with a garage selling old cars opposite.

We've been trying to get Helen's book back from Derek but he's already delivered it.

Who's Derek?

Derek delivers things to people who aren't there.

Who's Helen?

This is Helen. We've both escaped and I'm a Wanted Man and she's a Wanted Woman.

Don't bother wasting time putting a curse on me, says Helen, the doctors say I'm dying anyway.

You'd better have a bacon sandwich quick then, says the gypsy.

Helen whispers she doesn't think he's cast a spell on us yet.

How should I know? He could have done it already and we wouldn't know.

I whisper Do you feel any different, Helen?

Always. Do you?

I'm thinking hard. How are you meant to feel when you've been cursed by a gypsy? I tell Helen if he has cast a curse neither of us would know, because we'd both be different and wouldn't remember how we felt before. That's gypsy cunning.

I'm off to find a camp for the night now, he says. Like a lift?

We would and we do.

I'm sitting on the bench beside the gypsy with Helen on his horse, which is bonier than Aunt Beryl after she'd been on a food-free diet for a fortnight. An ambulance took her to hospital and she told the doctors she'd misread an article saying that gin contained all the human body needed for a happy, healthy life.

We're pulling the scooter behind the caravan.

Where are we going? I ask the gypsy. You haven't got a satnav to swear at.

Where the road takes us, the gypsy says.

Where's that?

Here, there, everywhere, who knows? That's the joy of travelling. He looks up and points and says The stars are my satnav.

I look up but there are no stars, it's just after lunch and the sun's out. Gypsies must have special eyes.

Late afternoon and we've arrived somewhere. We turn into a field.

This'll do. My horse needs a feed, the gypsy says.

Does the farmer know your horse is eating his grass?

He will in the morning. We'll be gone by then.

Then you're a thief and a criminal like us and detectives will Fit you Up like they're Fitting me Up, I tell him.

You can join our gang, says Helen.

The gypsy's drinking cans of beer then throwing them in the hedge, and going on and on about the joys of travelling and how perfect his gypsy life is. I pick off the ring pulls and add them to the necklace I've made for Sally.

I'm up with the lark, he says. I enjoy perfect freedom. I go where my fancy takes me, and if I like a place I stop and stay. I dine on the fruits of the hedgerows, and quaff Adam's ale.

I don't think Adam's ale comes in cans, whispers Helen, and nudges me. He's a fraud. I saw a Tesco supermarket bag in the caravan full of tins of Heineken.

It doesn't sound much of a perfect life to me. When you've got a horse you have to keep stopping to find grass. And as soon as you find any you have to leave before you get arrested for trespassing. Gypsies are a bit like Derek, they're never where they are because by the time they get there they have to leave. Being a gypsy isn't a perfect life like mine.

The gypsy makes another fire and we eat more bacon sandwiches.

When it's dark we go to the village pub. The man behind the bar says We don't serve gypsies. You'd better leave now.

We just want a drink, the gypsy says.

Men grab us by the shoulders. They punch the gypsy and a dog pees in his cap.

We're rumbling along looking for more grass. I ask the gypsy how he earns his money.

Odd jobs like gardening.

Gardening's not odd, I tell him. An odd job's mending nuclear power stations like the last Gentleman of the Road I met did. If you do gardening you must know what plants need sun and what plants need shade. I didn't when I worked in the garden centre, but it was no crisis.

No crisis for me, either, he says. By the time someone's plants wither and die I'm not there any longer. Anyway, my main line of business is designing B to B websites.

B&Bs with friendly faces like the one I stayed at in Minehead? I ask. It had fire doors and pipes in the walls that made noises and snakes wriggling through them.

He means Business to Business websites, says Helen.

I'm quick on the uptake and know about most things, but not websites. I know they live inside computers. But they also don't, because Bernhard said they're not actually inside computers, they live thousands of miles away at somewhere called Silicon Valley, which is even further than Scotland. And they're always racing off to a mast somewhere, and then to another mast somewhere else, before zapping all the way down to other people's computers like my words to Sally did.

Sally told Bernhard off about websites once. She told him to stop looking at you know what ones on her laptop and he laughed. You know you like them, Sally, he said, and she hit him again.

How do you design websites out here in the country? asks Helen. You've no wi-fi.

I hijack it. There's always someone with an easy password to crack. By the time they find out I've half-inched their bandwidth I'm in the next parish.

Let's see one of your websites, says Helen.

The gypsy turns on his laptop and presses some buttons.

What is a website? I ask.

It's a place on the internet that tells people what you're selling so they can buy it.

Like a shop? I ask.

A shop that's everywhere at once. This website here shows customers the advantages of buying plants and flowers from this supplier and not its competitors. People can browse its stock online even if they live in Africa or Australia.

I'm puzzled. Why would someone want to buy a plant from a shop in Australia? It would be dead by the time it arrived.

My websites create a powerful online presence, says the gypsy. They boost your profile, drive traffic to your business, and increase your ranking. Do you need one? Are you selling anything?

My abstract paintings, I tell him.

Perfect. I can make you a mobile friendly graphics-oriented site. You'd get full access to analytics and know precisely how many visitors browsed and which pages and paintings they looked at and for how long. And you're guaranteed increased ranking.

I tell the gypsy I don't think I want increased ranking, thank you. Not since I'm Trending and my hut became an example of an Open Plan Dynamic Interior. There may be hundreds of people visiting me at my Open Plan on Steroids hut at this very moment, so I don't want any more, even if I'm not there.

Helen's tapping buttons on the laptop. I've checked the analytics for your plant website, she says. It's got a raft of coding errors. And these links are broken, and I don't see much evidence of SEO or keyword placement. And the page ranking's not very high. Here, give me your mobile.

Helen taps buttons into my mobile and tells the gypsy his website's not mobile friendly, either. But that's no surprise. My mobile's not very friendly, either, I still can't speak to Sally through it.

Helen and I are bored hearing about the joys of travelling and going where the road takes us and looking for grass every evening and eating bacon sandwiches. We're off. The gypsy waves goodbye and travels on to where the road takes him.

We're resting for Twix time in an old pillbox by a canal.

Helen says she was lonely at the home.

I'm sad for her. I tell her I'm never lonely, I'm the best company for myself. I don't miss Billy, Nils and Nita, even if I am their parents in a way when I propagated them by bolting their parts together. Just like how mum bolted me together in her stomach.

Helen says she's pleased I helped her escape from the home. Especially as I'm an artist who's doesn't paint like Renoir and doesn't wear a string vest.

I tell her I like helping people and I'm glad I helped her. But it's important that you know how much they're being helped by other people before you help them. If everyone helped everyone else do everything, there'd be nothing left for them to do for themselves. And who's Renoir? I ask.

A dead Frenchman.

I thought you liked the French.

Not Renoir, he turned women into blubbery seals.

Helen's having a rest. I'm feeling a sudden Urge to do some measuring. I use one of Helen's crutches.

I measure the distance from the pillbox to the next bridge.

Then to the next bridge.

Then from the bridge to a lock.

Then from the lock to the next bridge.

Then between two posts by the path because I can't see any more bridges or locks.

I keep on measuring and I'm miles from Helen.

Back at last. I fell in the canal when a bike bumped into me under a bridge. The rider didn't stop.

I'm wet and cold and it's getting dark. This pillbox is made of concrete with slits for windows and was built in the War to kill invading Germans. I'm pointing one of Helen's crutches through the slits like a gun. But just for fun, the War's over, you have to be sensible about these things.

We can't stay here, says Helen, I've got standards. It's nasty horrible concrete and covered in disgusting graffiti, with loads of old beer cans and used condoms. Come on, we're moving on.

And we do.

Pillbox, a curious word. Mum had a pill box, but spelt with two words. She kept her pills in it. It had a picture of a Swiss castle on the lid. Dad didn't have one, he kept his pills in a beer mug in the drawer.

When they got old and kept forgetting what pills they'd swallowed I put all the different ones in plastic cups, one for each day of the week.

I picked them up from the chemist every week, and as mum and dad got older and older the bag of pills got bigger and bigger. If they hadn't gone into the Home I'd have been picking their pills up in a sack.

I put a blue pill into a plastic cup, then a white one, and then two red ones for Monday for dad.

Then another blue pill, then a white one, and then two red ones in another plastic cup for Tuesday.

Then another blue pill, then a white one, and then two red ones in another plastic cup for Wednesday.

Then another blue pill, then a white one, and then two red ones in another plastic cup for Thursday.

Then another blue pill, then a white one, and then two red ones in another plastic cup for Friday.

Then another blue pill, then a white one, and then two red ones in another plastic cup for Saturday.

Then another blue pill, then a white one, and then two red ones in another plastic cup for Sunday.

Then I did the same for mum.

It took me most of the morning.

When the pills from the doctor changed colour and

dad had two more pills and mum three more it took me all day. But I never complained, because mum and dad did so much for me, bringing me up and teaching me the wisdom that has helped me get where I am today. Which is here.

I don't think dad knew what day it was with his pills. Sometimes he swallowed Tuesday's pills on Thursdays, and Friday's on Sunday. I don't think they got to the right places inside him anyway, because he still ended up in the Home. Poor dad.

We find an old barn out in the fields. It's only got three sides but we snuggle up behind some hay bales. I check for goats, Helen for rats.

She asks me why I keep measuring everything.

I tell her that Dad told me The world's a big place, son, and you're a titch. There are things out there much bigger than you. But don't let appearances mislead. Some things may look big and threatening but they're actually small in stature. Get the measure of everything, and you'll know exactly where you are.

And I have, and he was right.

Time to clean my teeth before bed. Mum told me to clean my teeth every night. You need a good set of teeth to get a job, son, she said. Employers don't employ people with teeth missing. But she's in a Home now so I have to tell myself to clean them. Every night I imagine mum saying Do it now, son, clean them. And I do.

I've got good teeth thanks to mum. And they're in my mouth where teeth should be, unlike her's. Entertainers need good teeth because they have to smile all the time on the telly in close up.

Before we go to sleep Helen says Pass me my rabbit.

I've woken up and it's still dark. It's cold and I'm listening to Helen. She's making strange noises and moaning. I hope she's okay.

I don't know whether it's late in the night or early in the morning. So I'm consulting what doctors call my Internal Clock. It tells the parts of my body what time it is and what they should be doing or not doing, and whether I've had enough sleep and when it's time to wake up. Luckily, it doesn't ding the hours. If it did it would be embarrassing, especially in Company at midday when it dinged twelve times.

It's morning at last and I'm shivering. I didn't sleep much. I spent all night listening to Helen's strange noises and thinking about invading Germans. Germans still invade Britain but they're tourists, and want to visit Buckingham Palace rather than capture it.

We've come to a golf course. A lady and a man wearing jumpers covered in diamonds are playing. Her ball's stuck in a bunker and so is she.

She hits it up the sandy slope and it rolls back.
She hits it up the sandy slope and it rolls back.
She hits it up the sandy slope and it rolls back.
She hits it up the sandy slope and it rolls back.

The man looks cross.

She's using the wrong club, says Helen. She'd do better with a sand wedge.

Some people never learn, especially old people. And

it takes them all their lives to do it.

The lady hits her ball into the sand again and it rolls back.

The man's more angry than Uncle Pete with Aunty Vi when she threw away his jockstrap signed by David Seaman the Arsenal goalkeeper.

The lady gives her ball a big bash and falls over. It shoots out of the bunker, whizzes along the grass, and lands in the bushes. The man swears at her and says they'll have no chance in the mixed doubles if she plays like a bloody idiot. Not very nice. She's upset and gives him a V-sign when his back's turned. I would. They pick up their golf bags and go off to look for the ball.

They're old and the lady keeps dropping her golf bag.

She needs a caddy, says Helen. Look, I'm tired of walking on crutches, we need another scooter.

We can't steal one from an old person, I tell her. Old people need their scooters. If we took them they'd get stuck in their houses and have to slowly empty their fridges and eat corned beef with fungus on and rotten eggs and get stomach ache and die of starvation and not get found by their neighbours till six months after when only their skeletons were left with their faithful friends dead alongside them.

What about a golf buggy? says Helen. There'll be lots at the club house.

We can't steal one, I'm already a Wanted Man.

We'll borrow one, says Helen. We can drive it to the next golf club, leave it there, then borrow another. Then drive that to the next golf club, leave it, and borrow another. No problem, as all the golf clubs will end up with the same number of buggies.

186

But the first golf club will be a buggy short, I point out, as I'm very Quick on the Uptake.

We'll leave a note to tell the next golf club we left it at to drive it back to the golf club before, as they'll have an extra one. But we'll need to look like golfers, says Helen.

I'll borrow one of the lady's clubs while they're finding her ball, I say, she won't notice.

I creep across to the woman's golf bag, pull out a club, and run back.

We head through the trees towards the club house past a sign saying No 7 hole. 189 yards, par 3.

What does it mean? I ask.

It tells you how many yards to the hole. Your caddy measures the distance, tells you which club to use, and how hard to hit the ball.

I'm thinking. That sounds interesting, I like measuring. Maybe I'll be a caddy as well as an entertainer.

Go and steal a couple of golf jumpers, says Helen.

The club shop's packed with clubs and bags and golf balls and golf clothes and caps. When no one's looking I pull two jumpers with diamonds on off the hanger. In the changing room I put one of the jumpers on and then the other on top of that. They're a bit big, but it's no crisis. I walk out of the shop and no one notices because I look like a golfer.

The golf buggies are lined up against the wall. This one here's top of the range, says Helen. RXVs with three-phase induction, deep cycle batteries, coil springs, self-compensating pinion steering, scuff guards, and dual drinks holders. It'll do fifteen miles an hour. We'll be at the next golf club in no time. Jump in and start driving.

187

I can't drive, I tell her.

Nor could mum. She had fifty lessons and still went round a roundabout the wrong way. She caused a traffic accident and the instructor got broken legs and was flown to hospital in a helicopter.

You'll have to drive, says Helen, I can't. These buggies have got foot pedals and my legs don't work. Come on, turn that key. Push the switch there. Now press the pedal, and away we go.

And we do, but backwards not forwards. I jam on the brakes before we bash into the club house wall. I press a different switch and we're racing forwards. We're out of the gate and whizzing down the road and already breaking the sound barrier. This RXV is fast. I'm good at driving already.

We're Commanding the Road. We've built up a goods train behind us. I've tied the painting of nude Helen to the back of the scooter and drivers are hooting. A man pokes his head out of a van and shouts Ugly cow, but I'd give her one. Helen gives him a rude sign.

How do we find the next golf club? I ask.

Give me your mobile, says Helen. We'll use it as a satnav. She presses buttons and I'm surprised when a map of all the golf courses comes up on the screen. Had it been hiding there all along? I could have used the map to get to Budleigh Salterton. Even I find there are things to learn.

Turn left at the next junction, Helen says, it's precisely eight point six miles to the next club.

It's late afternoon and Helen's swearing at the mobile satnav like Derek. We've been to four golf clubs and borrowed four buggies.

Damn, says Helen, your mobile's run out of battery so we can't use the map any more. We must be close to your hut. Where is it?

I tell her how should I know? I've no idea where we are now.

We stop in a lay by for a Twix and a think.

Let's turn round and take the buggies back to where we started, I say. When we're there we'll know where we are again.

We drive to the last golf club we went to, give its buggy back, then drive the buggy we took from the one before that to the golf club before that.

At the second golf club we go to the buggy that we left. But it won't start because the battery hasn't got any electricity. So we take another one. I write a note to the golf club, because dad told me, Son, it's important to be honest.

I write The buggy we left here before we took the one that we've just brought back hasn't got any electricity. Please plug it in and feed it some electricity, then take it back to the golf club where we got it from. When you get there you'll find your own buggy and you'll have to plug that in and feed it some electricity before you drive it back here. It's no crisis.

I leave them a Twix. It's polite.

We're back walking again and we've stopped in a lay by. A car pulls in behind us and a man in a suit gets out and wees in the bushes.

He stares at my painting of Helen without any clothes

on. I'm staring at the damp stain on his trousers. That's not a wall painting, I tell him.

Interesting, he says, ignoring me and staring at the painting.

Helen says We're taking it to Sotheby's for a valuation. It's a family heirloom, a rare unsigned work by Kasimir Malevich. It was smuggled out of Russia by my ancestors to hide it from the Bolsheviks. Critics say it bears significant resemblances to Leger's tubular forms, and it's a classic example of Malevich's forays into Cubo-Futurism.

I like it, I'll buy it, says the man, and pulls out his wallet.

It's not for sale, says Helen.

I'll give you fifty pounds.

Make it a hundred, it's a deal.

Done. The man hands Helen his money and drives off with the painting. This'll pay for a hotel this evening, she says. I'm filthy. I need a shower and a decent night's sleep.

It's late afternoon and we're in a town. We stop outside an antiques shop and Helen says Wait here.

The window's full of old rubbish no one wants. Would I want a rusty old Hovis tin my white sliced would go mouldy in? I don't think so. Or an old clock that must have told Henry the Eighth the wrong time? Or a cracked mirror I can only see my left elbow in because the rest of it's covered in black spots? Who wants an old one of anything when they can have a new one? You have to be sensible.

Helen comes out and says she's sold a brooch her granny gave her for fifty pounds.

Further along the street she stops outside a charity shop and says Wait here. In the window are more vases with chips, broken plates, ornaments, and picture frames with no pictures in. It's like the antique shop but cheaper.

I've been waiting outside for ages. A lady comes out and says Come on, let's find a hairdresser.

I look round. Who's she talking to? I don't know her from Adam. Or Eve.

Come on, it's me.

I don't think so, I reply. Whoever you are.

It's me, she says, Helen.

And it is Helen. She's wearing a long dress with stars on and gold shoes with purple straps.

That's a pretty dress, I tell her. Sally's got one like it but green.

We stop outside a ladies' hairdresser. Wait here, she says.

The hairdresser's also what's called a Beautician. A sign says We offer ladies a wide range of superior beauty treatments, including fragrant manicures, power polish for hands and feet, gel varnish and gel removal, bikini line creation, eyelash extensions and infills, express facials, and full body spray tan.

I've been waiting outside for over an hour and a half and I'm bored. A lady comes out.

Come on, she says, let's find a hotel.

I look round but I can't see who she's talking to.

It can't be Helen, This lady's got golden skin, eyelashes as long as a cow, and pink stripes in her hair.

It's me, says Helen.

Even though I don't recognise her, it is.

You look lovely, Helen. A bit plump, but lovely. Like the ladies in magazines. I like your tan. It must be hot as the Bahamas in that shop for you to turn brown like that.

I went for the quick action full body spray, maximum toning and a facial. And a leg waxing.

Which leg? Won't the other one look different?

You really are a Neanderthal, she says.

Another compliment.

Come on, let's find a hotel room, I need a shower.

At what's called the Premier Inn Helen tells the lady we want a twin room. The lady says No problem, madam, and gives us a key. We go down a long corridor, through a fire door, down another long corridor, through another fire door, and down another very long corridor to room 126. It's got two beds and not much else. Helen has a shower and I watch a programme on the telly about a man inside a fish tank having spiders dropped on his head while everyone laughs. Then I watch more people having ants and worms crawling all over their faces and everyone laughs again.

When I wanted to get into the bathroom Helen was sitting on the toilet throwing a toilet roll tube into the waste basket. But she kept missing. She said a tube's totally not aerodynamic. I said Give it to me. I sat on the toilet and threw it and it went straight in. Helen looked cross and threw me out.

I'm dying to do a number two but Helen's Hogging the Bathroom which Sally often did. Once Bernhard said I'll hog it with you, Sally, and they didn't come out for an hour.

I'd like to Hog the Bathroom with Sally, but not with Bernhard.

I've just woken up and a lady comes out of the bathroom and drops her towel. She's naked.

I'm feeling another sudden Urge. It must be Helen who's come out because it was Helen who went in. She's golden all over like the lady in the James Bond film and looks beautiful, even with the beard between her legs.

Do I look desirable? she asks, and lies on the bed.

I think so, I tell her. A bit plump.

I haven't looked desirable since I left Budleigh Salterton. They wouldn't let me look desirable at the home. What was the point? The doctor I fancied had to keep a professional distance even though I know he wanted to ravish me. You're not my type at all, but I hope you'll ravish me just to get things going.

When Helen's not looking I look up Ravish in my dictionary. It says To seize and carry off by force. But I already have ravished her when I helped her escape from the home and carried her for miles. But I didn't have to seize or force her to let me do it. I'm puzzled.

In the restaurant I eat sausages and chips and chocolate ice cream and a meringue.

Helen says, Let's go to the bar, I need a drink.

She buys two scotch drinks. Mine tastes like cough medicine, but I'm feeling better than I did before I drank it.

She orders two more scotch drinks and I feel even better, but a bit tired. They should give scotch drinks to patients feeling ill at surgeries.

I'm dropping off, which is not very polite when you're with a lady.

Helen says Go to bed, I'll be up later. You can ravish me then.

Which is even more curious. Where does she want to be carried off to by force now? We've got a room for the night here.

Morning, I've woken up. Where's Helen? Her bed hasn't been slept in. I go down the long corridor, through the fire door, down another long corridor, through another fire door, and along a long corridor to the reception.

Where's Helen? I ask the lady.

Helen who? I've just come on shift. There's a lady in the restaurant, that could be her.

I go in and there's Helen. She's eating breakfast with a man. He's wearing a tiny string vest with Rogue Hunk written on it in big letters. His nipples peep out at the sides. Every time he reaches for his toast massive muscles like cauliflowers poke out of his arms. His legs are tree trunks. I've seen smaller gorillas at the zoo.

This is Dean, she says.

Hello Dean, I say.

Dean doesn't say much. He's too busy eating two Full English Breakfasts and drinking four cups of tea.

That was lovely, he says, licking his lips. As are you, my little flower, and he touches Helen between her legs, which is quite rude.

Helen squeals and says Naughty!

Dean's a real man, she whispers to me, and looks up at

him and strokes his knee.

Right, time to leave, she says. We're off.

Can I have my breakfast first? I ask her.

Not you, just me and Dean.

Where are you going? I ask.

North in Dean's BMW M3. It's the twin-turbo 3-litre inline-6 model, making 425 horsepower and 406 lbs torque with a seven-speed dual clutch. And it's red and thrusting like Dean. I want sex, and lots of it before I die. Everything's working perfectly apart from my legs. She smiles at Dean and he smiles back and pats her bottom.

Dean doesn't say very much but he seems nice. Unlike Bernhard, who wasn't.

Goodbye Helen, I say. I'm glad everything's working apart from your legs.

Dean's car's breaks the sound barrier across the car park, and something flies out of the window as it races out on to the road to the North. The something bounces across the ground and lands at my feet. It's Helen's rabbit. I pick it up and run after her.

Come back, Helen, you've dropped your rabbit! One of your most important things!

She doesn't hear me, she's gone. Poor Helen, she'll be sad when she finds out. I'll use it for measuring things.

Without Helen I'm bored being a Wanted Man. I've decided to throw myself on the Fair Play of British Justice.

I find a police station and tell the sergeant at the desk I've come to give myself up.

Take a seat, sir, he says.

I sit down next to a man in a string vest. He's covered in tattoos, more than the man and lady in the camper van had who tattooed Sally on my stomach. The man's tattoos aren't friendly like mine. He's got snakes wriggling down his arms, monster faces on his chest, and I Heart My Mother on his forehead. I step on his foot by mistake and he glares and shows his fists. One hand's got Love tattooed on the fingers and the other Hate. This man needs to know I'm a criminal too and not someone to be messed with, so I tell him I've got a tattoo, too.

I pull up my jumper. It's meant to be Sally, I tell him, but it looks more like Aunt Megs, who's old and dead. Helen said it's more like a map of Venezuela or the Orinoco estuary.

Cool. What you in for then, bro?

I'm giving myself up before I get Fitted Up by the police.

Giving yourself up? That's a dumb ass thing to do, believe old Andy. Me, I'm done for nicking motors, cruising the manor in Beamers. I wear turtles on a job, but I'd had a few jars, got a bit clever and left them off.

Turtles? I'm puzzled.

Gloves, man. Filth found my dabs on the gear knob and I was well and truly screwed.

Me, I tell him, I'm being Fitted Up because the filth found me with a gun.

Growler crime, eh? You're going down big time, bro. Some choice advice from old Andy. Get yourself a decent brief. And when they bang you up steer clear of Charlie Big Spuds. There's one in every nick. And believe me, bro, he'll have your pants down. Nark to the screws, they'll turn a blind eye. Man, I'm parched. A mug of diesel and two sugars would go down nicely.

I'm puzzled. I need a decent brief, whatever that is.

And I have to steer clear of Charlie Big Spuds. He must be the prison gardener. Prisoners grow vegetables inside, it's called Rehabilitation.

The policeman comes over. This way, sir. He takes me along a corridor, through a metal door, along another corridor, through another metal door and into a tiny room.

Two detectives give me the Once Over. They switch on a tape recorder.

One of them says Time 17 minutes past nine. Present are D I Jacks and D I Logan.

So, what can we do you for, sir?

I'm a Wanted Man and I've come to give myself up. I'm throwing myself on the Fair Play of English Justice.

A bit rash. What crime have you committed, sir?

I got caught with a growler.

Gun crime, eh? Hmm, serious. And this alleged offence occurred where precisely, sir?

Budleigh Salterton. I went there to return Helen's book, but I left it in Derek's van and he delivered it to the house where Helen doesn't live any more, and I helped her escape from the home, and she's dying and doesn't need her hamster book any more because she wants sex, lots of it before she dies, and ...

Slow down, chummy. Tell us about this firearm.

The man in the sports car I got a lift from planted it on me then grassed.

It's best to talk in police language in a police station.

And I want a decent brief.

You'll get the duty solicitor and like it, matey.

I don't want to go down, I tell them. Especially if the screws let Charlie Big Spuds pull my pants down. My pants are private.

Nothing's private inside, son. You seem to know a lot about being inside. Not your first offence, is it?

I shake my head, I'm saying nothing.

For the tape, is that a yes or no?

I haven't committed an offence, so don't try to Fit Me Up, I tell them.

We'll see about that, sonny.

I'm parched. Any chance of a mug of diesel and three sugars?

You'll get refreshments when we're done. Being caught in the possession of an illegal firearm's a serious offence. Run a search, Bob, and get him a brief. For the tape, D I Logan has left the room. Right, son, my colleague's checking if you've got a record.

We're waiting.

The detective comes back and D I Jacks says D I Logan enters the room. They look at a sheet of paper.

Right, sir, you can go.

Go where? I'm not being Fitted Up?

You're free to go, sonny. It wasn't your gun, it was the driver's.

Is that because he wasn't wearing turtles like the man in the string vest outside and you had his dabs on file?

He's a known villain. Record as long as your arm. You were free to go at the Budleigh station, but you'd left before they had the chance to tell you.

So I never was a Wanted Man?

Goodbye, sir.

Phew. We go back through the metal door, along a corridor, through another metal door, and into the reception area.

The man with the tattoos looks up.

Where you off to, bro?

I'm free to go, I tell him. I didn't need a Decent Brief after all.

You must have pull. Respect, bro. High Five.

I tell him I hope it's not his pants Charlie Big Spuds pulls down when he gets banged up, and he glares at me and shows his fists.

I'm standing on the police station steps outside doing what Wanted Men who aren't wanted any more do on the telly - enjoying the Air of Freedom. But it's cloudy and drizzly and I'm thirsty. I'm off to get a mug of diesel and a Twix.

I'm imagining I'm back in the combe near my hut talking to the robin on the oak tree. People think robins are friendly. Not me. Robins aren't friendly at all. The magpies in the combe steal their eggs, cracking the shells and gobbling the yolks so there are no babies. Which makes the robins very cross, and because of their irresistible Urge they have to Propagate again, which is a chore, especially for the lady robins, who have to squeeze eggs through a very tiny hole in their bottoms.

Which must be painful.

Sally saw a robin when we did my number 3 Prune walk. She said Isn't he a cutie? And doesn't he sing beautifully. I'd like to cuddle him.

I said Yes he is, Sally, because I didn't want to upset her. People think birds sing because they're happy, but they're really shouting and swearing at us. My robin spent most of the day shouting at me in a singing voice saying Push off, I live here, not you!

Birds kill each other all the time. The Reverend Des says they're all God's children, though, and part of the Wonder of Creation.

Aunt Megs liked birds. She had a budgie called Budge. She said Ain't my Budge pretty?

I don't think so, I told her. I gave Budge a look in the eye and then in the other eye, and neither looked friendly or pretty. She let Budge out of its cage once when we went to Sunday dinner, and it flew round and round the room and pooed on dad's head. We could see the specks because dad didn't have much hair. No one told him, and Aunt Megs laughed.

I told her Budge didn't mean us any good at all. And she got cross when I said Budge's face looked cruel, like the pictures in granddad's National Geographics of primitive savages who cut off explorers' heads and roasted them on camp fires.

Your Budge is a primitive savage, I told her, and she went into a huff and hid the biscuits.

I've been hitching. A man stops and gives me a lift. He's taking me to see mum and dad. His old car doesn't go much faster than Helen's scooter. It smells of faithful friends and it rattles, and my window keeps dropping down. The car makes blow-off noises every time we stop at traffic lights.

The driver doesn't imagine they're green like Helen, he waits till they are, which is probably sensible, because by the time we've crawled to the other side of the crossing they're already red again.

He doesn't give me a gun, just wine gums. Two were

orange, but it was no crisis.

I'm at mum and dad's Home.

I'm waiting at the door. I've rung the bell twice but no one answers. Waiting's a waste of valuable time. Dad told me if he added up all the time he'd waited for mum outside public toilets he could have flown to the moon.

But not back, I hope, Mum whispered. She's got very good ears.

I'm too busy to wait, so I creep round the side past windows with net curtains. They're all shut tight so I can't climb in. Old people need heat, lots of it, even in summer. Round at the back there's an open door. I creep inside and smell cauliflower. I'm in the kitchen.

I creep along like I'm a criminal again.

In the first room an old lady's asleep. She may be dead, but how should I know, I'm not a doctor. I hope not, she looks like someone's mum, and I wouldn't want my mum dead. She's left most of her prunes and custard.

The door to the next room's open. An old man's asleep. He doesn't look much like dad. He's left most of his prunes and custard too.

The door to the next room's closed so I knock.

No answer.

I knock again.

No answer.

Knocking on old people's doors is usually a waste of time, because most are deaf and wouldn't hear it anyway.

I start looking for old men wearing odd socks like dad does. But some of them are in bed so I can't see.

I knock on one old man's door and he shouts out I need to go!

I don't think so. There's a very nasty smell so I think he's been already.

Another old man shouts You're not getting my money, you bastards!

Room nineteen's empty and the telly's on. I watch a very pretty lady shaking white dust all over a carpet. She sucks it all up in a hoover and gives me a big smile. Then she shakes more dust on the carpet and sucks it up with a different hoover. And smiles at me again. She's nice. She does it four times with different hoovers. Then a clock appears on the screen and the time goes down and down and down until it says in big letters Going, Going Gone.

And that's it. I'm not surprised no one's watching, I wouldn't.

I've looked inside lots of rooms but can't find mum and dad. It's ages since I've visited because the bus goes everywhere before it gets to the Home so I usually phone. I'm not really sure what mum and dad look like now. When people get old you can't always recognize them. All old ladies have white hair and look like the Queen. And they never know it's you because they haven't got their glasses on.

I need a nurse to help me find mum and dad. The last room's empty and I'm tired, so I lie down for a rest. It's Twix time.

A nurse comes in. What are you doing in here? How did you get in?

I've come to see mum and dad, but I can't find them.

Whose mum and dad is that?

Mine.

We've lots of mums and dads. Whose do you want to visit?

Just mine this time. I'm too busy to visit the others.

She looks cross.

And you are?

Their son.

She looks crosser. Look, I need to know your parents' names.

Trevor and Eileen.

Ah, their room's next door. Or was. Look, you'd better sit down. I'm so sorry, but I'm afraid I've some bad news for you. Your dad passed away a fortnight ago. We've been trying to contact you, but we'd no address.

That's because I've been away from my hut, trying to give Helen back her book, but I couldn't because Derek had it in his delivery van and he's delivered it to Budleigh Salterton where Helen doesn't live any more, and she's escaped and could be anywhere having lots of sex with a man called Dean.

I'm very sorry for your loss.

Poor dad. I'm feeling very sad, very sad indeed, and I'm crying. She puts her arm round me and I cry some more.

I ask her When's the funeral?

You've missed it, I'm afraid. Mum isn't here, either. She was taken poorly and she's in hospital. I can give you the ward number. We've kept dad's things for you, they're in this box.

I rummage through it.

I don't want his turnup trousers, I tell the nurse, I wear turnips. Or his braces.

No problem, we can dispose of it all for you.

I'd like his odd socks.

Of course. Is there anything else we can do for you at

this difficult time?

Can I have some prunes and custard?

Poor dad, I'm very sad. I'll visit mum in hospital. She must be sad too.

I'm at the hospital. I ask the lady at reception where I can find her.

We've over a thousand patients, dear. Name?

Eileen.

I'll need more than that to find her.

I tell the lady that mum was in the home but got ill and was sent here to get better. Dad's just died and I missed his funeral because I was returning Helen's book but couldn't because it was in Derek's van. The nurse at the home said mum's in ward B2.

Ah, you should have told me that first, dear. I'm very sorry for your loss.

She taps letters into her computer. You'll find your mum in Zone C, ward C3.

This hospital's big. It's got a shop selling newspapers, magazines and flowers. I buy a Twix and a bunch of roses for mum. Mums like flowers.

I push through fire doors then go up some stairs. At the top there are more fire doors. I hold them open for a nurse who's running very fast along the corridor. She looks busy like all nurses. I hope no one's been shot with a growler. Shooting people makes nurses busy in hospitals and they're busy enough already.

I'm walking along a very long corridor. I can't see to

the end, so it could go on for ever. A blue sign says Zone A. Which way now?

I smell cauliflower. And disinfectant. And polish. The floors are shiny and there are paintings on the walls. They're all show pretty fields and flowers and horses and they're not Abstract at all, so I won't have an exhibition here.

I pass Oncology, Cardiology, Immunology, Pathology, and Radiology. Phew. Lots of things with long names that go wrong with people. The patients in bed here can't be very well at all.

I go through more fire doors and see a blue sign saying Zone B. Patients are lying on trolleys in the corridor and looking fed up. It's busy. Everyone's got pyjamas on, even the doctors and nurses. The doctors wear green pyjamas and the nurses blue ones. They've all got what are called Crocs on like Sally's, and they're all in a hurry going somewhere to make people better from all the illnesses with long words.

I walk past Neurosciences, Burns Unit, Plastic Surgery, Endoscopy and Paediatrics. This is definitely not a healthy place to be, so I stuff toilet paper up my nose, you can't be too careful.

I go along another long corridor I can't see the end of. Past Acute Medicine, Antenatal Care, Aortic Surgery, and Cardiology.

Then through more fire doors past Radiology, Pathology, Immunology, Cardiology, and Oncology.

I think I've been here before. I'm back in Zone A.

I go into the shop and buy another Twix. Time to start again.

This time I turn left not right. Nurses are pushing very ill people in trolleys up and down the corridors. I pass Chemotherapy and Gastroenterology, go through more fire doors, up more stairs, through more fire doors past Microbiology. I hold the doors open for more busy nurses who say Thank you as they rush by. Then along another corridor.

I'm in Zone D. I go along the corridor, turn left, go through more fire doors, passing Renal Unit, Speech and Language Therapy, Stroke Services.

Phew. I go through more fire doors, past Day Unit to another blue sign saying Zone C.

I go up to a desk. Nurses and doctors are sitting at computers, talking on phones, and writing in coloured pens on a big board.

I wait, which is polite. These people are busy making people better. They're using computers instead of just giving them operations and pills. Which is one of the Wonders of Modern Medicine.

I've been waiting ages but no one has looked up saying Can I help you?

I say Excuse me. No one looks up. I say Excuse me, louder. No one looks up.

At last a nurse says Can I help you?

I tell her I've come to see Eileen my mum. The nurse says Ah, she's in ward C3. Go down there, turn left, and it's the third ward along.

I'm in mum's ward. It's full of people looking very ill. They're all asleep or staring at the ceiling. I wonder if they're achieving Eternal Peace. One's snoring, another's reading a paper upside down, and there are curtains round one of the beds.

I can't see mum. I peek through curtains and see a lady having something done to her bottom parts. It's not mum.

The beds have name tags above them. This one's mum's. It says Nil by Mouth. Aunt Megs ate everything Nil by Mouth. She did have a mouth, but because her throat didn't work any more she had to eat through her stomach. Mum's not in her bed.

I go back to the desk and wait ages again till a nurse notices me.

Where's Eileen, my mum? I ask her.

Mum's gone to the theatre, she says. You can wait here to see her when she gets back if you like. Nothing to worry about, mum's fine.

That's a relief, I was very worried. Mum can't be that ill if she's gone to an afternoon matinée. I hope it's a musical and she's well enough to have popcorn. She likes Gilbert O'Sullivan.

There are magazines on the table. They're called Wild Glamping, Tasteful Living, Desirable Lifestyles, Pec Building for the Modern Dude, Luxury Yachts, Performance Cars, English Country Gardens. I pick up one called Dynamic Interiors. It's the October edition, which is curious as it's only just September. Inside are pictures of lots of houses and rooms. There are adverts where you can buy a table made out of railway sleepers for £5,250, a kitchen tap for £1,500, and a table lamp for £960. I don't think so.

I turn the pages and there's my room.

I'm looking at Billy, Nils and Nita.

I'm surprised.

In fact I'm shocked.
What do the words say?

A milestone in simple living

Turn off a Somerset country lane, pick your way along a muddy woodland path, avoiding the renegade gate that dropped on our photographer's foot, pass a trio of enticing forks in the trail, and you will arrive at a secret woodland home.

The young abstract artist owner of this rural hideaway is as elusive as the woodland birds that peck at the windows. What do we know about him? Only that he prefers to remain nameless and is glimpsed only rarely, limping down the track to the village. Cornelius Hardaker, his close friend and dealer, insists that anonymity and solitude are vital components of his art.

This simple stable home, formed of weathered and bleached lapped panels, is a thrilling exercise in uncluttered living, and a triumph of formal restraint. Peer through the window and you will see a living space that interior designer Eddie van Yip quips is open plan on steroids. Push open the juddering door and you can imagine yourself back in the old rustic stable, where a pony once stamped its feet and drew hay from a suspended byre, now in use as a storage shelf.

Our artist worked with no fixed plan to conjure this basic shelter, and it seems to have grown organically, contingent only on the fundamental demands of eating, sleeping and painting. The only concessions to the modern world are a duo of classic pieces of flat pack furniture. These Ikea favourites, including the iconic Billy bookcase, combine masterfully, underlining the essential introspection of the flowing space. The Nils chair has been cleverly converted to a serviceable coffee table.

The carpet of flattened cardboard boxes cunningly articulates the open space, and confirms the artist's commitment to recycling. Pad around and the powerful spirit of place is tangible. In its very inconspicuousness it is conspicuous.

The whole is a timely exercise in creative reduction, and a refreshing demonstration of the fundamental essence of uncomplicated domestic living. The unforced style disguises painstaking thought, its reclusive inhabitant approaching interior design as an exercise in what to leave out. The result both is and is not ascetic.

I'm Trending. In a big way. How many magazines do they sell? There could be hundreds of people looking through the windows of the hut at this moment. And how did they know I'm an Abstract Artist?

I need to get back to the hut – and quick. As the nurse said mum's fine and enjoying a musical I'll visit her when she's back from the matinée.

I'm walking back along the track through the combe to get to the hut.

There are lots of things I want to do that I haven't been doing while I've been not returning Helen's book. I want to search through my microscope for more tiny creatures with waving legs. I want to be a pile of leaves again, and I want to talk to Billy, Nils and Nita. They'll have missed me.

The sun's come out. I'm standing by the stream watching it dusting the pebbles. I still don't know whether sunlight dusts. The stream's just the same as it was before I left, but different, as it always is, flowing past the old mill out to the sea where it will still be water but with salt. Before it got to the combe it had dropped out of the sky as rain from clouds, and before then it was probably dangerous rapids in the Orinoco estuary full of crocodiles and giant swimming snakes that David Attenborough makes friends with. Then it flew all the way across the Atlantic in clouds then fell again as rainwater in the stream.

The stream's still splashing light. And there's a stick snagged on a rock. Is it bent? Can water make a stick bend? I still don't know so I'll need to do more investigating. I'm going to be busier than ever.

There are things I want to measure in the combe, like how far it is from the ant hill to the hut. And the distance from the holly tree to the fallen oak. I'll use Helen's rabbit as a measurer. The distances will be different, but they'll still be a rabbit and bit, or a rabbit and two bits, but different. But in reality they'll still be the same distance in External Reality whatever stick I use. Or will they? Questions, questions. It's making me think hard, so maybe I will become a philosopher. I can see why they never run out of questions.

So much to do and think about in my busy life.

I've decided there are more intriguing things here in

the combe than in all the other places I've been to. I'm pleased to be back.

Here's where I was a mouse for a day. And I've just passed a lady hiker and she said Good Morning and I said Good Morning but just after she did so I didn't interrupt. I didn't try to catch her eye, because I want to get back to the hut as fast as possible to see Billy, Nils and Nita.

I'm just coming up to the hut and there's a crowd of people outside. They're not ramblers as they're not wearing bright anoraks and woolly hats.

They're standing talking on the path just where I turn off to the hut. What are they saying? I creep along behind them through the trees.

I'm hiding behind the holly where I can hear them.

Incredible, says a man in a pink jumper and tight trousers and gel in his hair.

Dynamic, says another, wearing a green shirt, red tie, and long pointy shoes covered in mud.

It's certainly open plan on steroids, like the magazine said.

The whole set up's a milestone in reduced living.

A triumph of restraint.

The spirit of place is almost tangible.

In its very inconspicuousness it's conspicuous.

Refreshing, too, a bold exercise in what to leave out.

Paradoxically, it both is and isn't ascetic.

There's the art!

So, where is our anonymous artist?

Apparently, he comes, he goes, and no one knows.

Lives a monk's existence by the sounds of it.

A bit of a hermit. I bet you a fiver he's got a beard down to his ankles.

And probably wears a bit of old sacking.

Curiously, his very lack of presence accentuates the essential introspection of the flowing space.

The men rub dust off the windows and peer inside the hut.

There's Billy, just like in the magazine photos. And Nils the chair he uses as a table.

Existence pared down almost beyond the quick.

Gasp provoking.

And destined to be a place of pilgrimage for all radical interior designers.

Lucky we're here early, ahead of the crowd.

Only just. See there? More coming up the path.

Pub time? Pannini?

I'm seriously Trending. It's time to leave.

Mr Hardaker must have told everyone in the world I'm an Abstract Artist. I'd better go and find out what he's done with my paintings.

I dodge two more people on the track to the village. They're carrying copies of the magazine and talking about my hut.

At Mr Hardaker's a green flag's flying.

I knock.

Who's that knocking? Come in if you must whoever you are, I can't get to the door.

I push the door open. Mr Hardaker's throwing dice again. He doesn't look round.

You saw the flag?

Yes.

The red one?

The green one.

My red flag's green?

Yes.

It's meant to be red. Green means I'm in, red I'm out. Look, I've got a lot on. If I'd heard you coming I'd have nipped out and changed the flags over.

It's me.

Ah, you again, my limping friend.

I'm Trending, I tell him.

You are indeed. Courtesy of yours truly earning my very reasonable seventy percent. Plus expenses, of course, of which I'm making a list.

I don't want to be Trending, Mr Hardaker. My hut's surrounded by people.

Never kick against the pricks, my friend. Most artists would die for the exposure and publicity I've got for you.

Where are my paintings?

I've organised a one-man exhibition.

An exhibition where?

Rawson's.

Not Mr or Mrs Rawson the sculptor? He or she's never there. I won't sell anything because it'll be shut all the time.

We'll hold a Private View. A personal appearance by the artist invariably galvanises the tills. Come on, let's get off to Rawson's. I'll forgo the world of chance and seriality and don my agent's hat.

Can I wear your goggles?

We're off. We're skidding round corners breaking the

Sound Barrier. We must be back at Budleigh Salterton. But we're not, we're racing up the hill to Mr or Mrs Rawson's church.

We're there already. It's only three miles from the hut, which is curious.

Inside, the sculptor's hitting a lump of stone with a mallet. I'm already choking, his or her church is even more dusty than last time.

Mr Hardaker yells Drop that vorpal blade, Rawson. Time to address Abstract Art at its most primitive and saleable.

The sculptor drops his chisel and chokes. You look like a grounded trout, my friend, says Mr Hardaker.

He or she wipes her hands on his apron and says Tea, anyone?

We're drinking tea from jam jars and eating soggy biscuits.

Just look at these paintings, Rawson. Outstanding, eh? I've agreed a very reasonable seventy percent agent's fee, and there's ten for you if we hang our friend's paintings in the vestry. The dust will bring them a useful patina.

We're hanging the pictures in the vestry. It's a bit cramped. Mr Hardaker has hung two of my landscapes and three of the ugly ladies upside down, but it's no crisis.

Right, he says, let's go and put up some posters.

I'm back in the sidecar and we're racing through the countryside. Mr Hardaker keeps jamming on the brakes and I leap out and nail posters on trees and notice boards.

That should do the trick, says Mr Hardaker.

Today. No one comes.

Tomorrow, which is now today. No one comes.

The day after tomorrow which is also now today, but a more recent one. No one comes.

I had more customers in the lay by, I tell Mr Hardaker.

Patience, my trending friend. It took Van Gogh years to be appreciated.

We drink more tea from jam jars while the sculptor works on another Immortal Plinth.

The roar of an engine outside. At last, a customer.

A van drives into the field below the church and churns mud. Mr Hardaker hurries out. I hear swearing from the cab.

Welcome, welcome, says Mr Hardaker. You're privileged to be the first to enjoy this exhibition of the very finest in abstract art. Come in and have tea and cake and browse.

It's Derek.

Still swearing, Derek kicks his van and we go into the church and through to the vestry.

Well, here they are. What do you think? Outstanding, aren't they. Primitive, and so atavistic they come out the other side. And everyone a bargain.

Derek is staring at my ugliest woman painting. You like that one? says Mr Hardaker. Yours for just £250.

I'll take it, Derek says. It'll remind me of my fucking satnav lady. I'm selling the van and becoming a male model. He hands over his money and heads off to churn more mud.

I liked his satnav lady. I'll miss her.

Told you, said Mr Hardaker, grinning at me. You've

just earned £12.50.

I'm at Sally's, knocking on her door. I hear what I think is called Heavy Metal Groove and not Sally's screamy Japanese music. A man in a dressing gown answers.

Is Sally doing your washing too? I ask him.

Sally who?

Sally who lives here.

There's no Sally living here. I'm Josh, and there's Chris, Karen and Holly, but no Sally.

Are you sure?

Sure I'm sure, mate. Now, if we're done you'll have to excuse me, I'm having a shower.

Do you know where Sally is?

She must have moved out.

Where to?

How should I know, chum? I'm just sofa surfing for a few nights. The others are at work. He shuts the door on me.

How can I find Sally now? There are thousands of houses here and she could have moved to Scotland where there are thousands more. I'll ring her on my mobile. I press buttons and numbers.

Hello, Sally, it's me. Where are you? Over.

I sit in a cafe and eat a cream tea.

My mobile shivers in my pocket and buzzes. It's a message.

Who r u?

Poor Sally, she still can't spell. I hope she's found a job where it doesn't matter. But not bricklaying or being a bin lady, she wouldn't like that. And nor would I.

I go back to her old flat and knock again. I hear more Heavy Metal music inside. The same man comes to the door.

You again.

Yes, it's me. Can I speak to Chris, Karen or Holly?

Wait here.

A pretty girl comes to the door.

I'm Holly. Sally moved out. I've got her forwarding address, but I'm not sure I should be giving it to you.

I'm Sally's friend, she'll want to see me. I've been away.

Chris, Karen and the man wearing the dressing gown all come to the door and stare at me.

Who are you, anyway? says Holly.

Sally's my friend. We share jokes and laugh together and eat jammy dodgers. I've been away from my hut, trying to give Helen back her book, but I couldn't because Derek had it in his van and he's delivered it to Budleigh Salterton where she doesn't live any more, and she's escaped and could be anywhere having lots of sex with a man called Dean.

They're whispering together, like Billy, Nils and Nita.

Holly says We don't feel inclined to give you Sally's address, we think you're a bit weird. She shuts the door, which I think is very rude.

People are odd.

I've been to Sally's mum's house. She hadn't moved. Luckily, she remembered me, and then said she wasn't sure she should give me Sally's new address either.

Sally told me her mum likes a good chat. So I sat on

her sofa until it was quite dark drinking tea and eating biscuits. I told her all about my travels trying to return Helen's book, and about all the people I met, and about shopping for bargains at the supermarket and ordering my Indian. I showed her my tattoo and she agreed it didn't look like Sally at all, and asked me why I got it done in the first place. I told her Sally's my favourite person, and we tell jokes and laugh together. And how I was glad Bernhard had left her, even after she was kind enough to do his washing when I went round and saw him wearing just his underpants. I said I want to get back to living in my hut and measuring lots of stuff again, and I show her Helen's rabbit.

And I told her I was worried Sally can't spell properly and she won't be able to get a job and I want to see her so I can help teach her.

Sally's mum said Actually, Sally's got eight O levels and an A level in English, and looked cross.

We had another cup of tea and some rich tea biscuits.

Sally's mum kept sighing and looking at her watch. Finally she said Look, you win, I might as well give it to you, I'm late for my zumba class.

Zumba? It's probably African cake icing or cooking the Zambian way. It's what ladies do who are Sally's mum's age and feeling that Life is Passing Them By because their children have left home.

I'm knocking on Sally's new door. I can hear scratchy, screamy Japanese music inside so she must be in. The door opens.

Hello, Bernhard.

Christ, it's you. Sally, Micro Man's turned up.

Bernhard's wearing just his underpants again. That's Sally all over, still doing his washing even though he left her but has come back. She's kind.

Sally comes to the door in her nightie, which is quite see through.

Hello, stranger. You'd better come in.

I'm sitting on Sally's sofa listening to scratchy, screamy Japanese music and eating jammy dodgers.

Sally and Bernhard are making noises in the bedroom.

I'm happy, it's good to be back.